THEIR FOREVER HOME

The American West Series

LAURA STAPLETON

Text and Cover Image Copyright © 2020 Laura L Stapleton

Cover by Cheeky Covers

Edited by Aquila Editing

All Rights Reserved.

No portion of this book may be reproduced, stored in a retrieval system, or transmitted in any form or by any means, mechanical, electronic, photocopying, recording, or otherwise, without written permission from the author or publisher.

Names, characters, and some incidences are imaginary and complete fiction. The places are real whenever possible, and some geographical names have been changed since the story took place.

CHAPTER 1

Quincy Easton held tight to the two boys' hands. Guiding them through Omaha, Nebraska's train station didn't take all his effort. Still, he wanted to be sure they reached the train platform on time. Jacob and Michael Anderson were his last two children to find families for, and they already had possible parents. The youngest one, Jacob, or Jake for short, lagged behind, so Quincy scooped him up. Light for a three-year-old, carrying him was easy.

"Mike?" he said, and the boy looked up from the floor at him. "How're you doing?"

Michael gave him a side-eye glance. "Good. Glad I'm not a baby like some people are."

Jake leaned over and blew a raspberry. Quincy laughed. "All right. No fighting. Let's get to the train first." He held on to Mike's hand a little tighter as they entered a narrower part of the station. People of all sorts walked toward them, fresh off of a newly arrived train. Those from larger cities ignore him while the small-town folks always grinned. If he had his choice, he'd move somewhere far smaller than his current home in Chicago.

After a few twists and turns, they reached the outside walkway. Smells of a cowtown city mixed with the fresh spring air. The strap on his bag dug into his shoulder with each step. He'd be glad to get these two into their seats for a short nap if the smoothness of the tracks allowed.

Mike tried to pull free. Quincy held tight, saying, "Stay with me," before seeing the reason for the boy's attempted escape. A large rain puddle stood between them and the train car's door. Unlike the inner city, this water was fresh from a passing morning storm. He let go of the boy, laughing when he hopped in with both feet. "You'll have to sleep sockless after lunch, you know."

Without a pause in splashing, Mike quipped, "It's all right, Mr. Easton. I'm washing my feet."

Jake began squirming. "I wanna wash mine." He wriggled, sliding down Quincy's hip and leg.

"Fine." Two sets of socks and shoes would take as long as one set to dry. He let go of Jake, who began hopping up and down with his brother in the puddle. The passersby either ignored the stomp fest or looked on disdainfully before boarding. When the whistle sounded, Quincy stepped forward, reaching his hands to both boys. "We need to go, or we'll miss our train. Your new parents will think you've changed your mind if we don't arrive on time."

Distracted by the possibility of losing a forever home, Jake and Mike took hold of Quincy's hands. He led Jake onto the train first, helping him with a lift up when the boy jumped. Then Mike hopped on by himself with Quincy bringing up the rear. He'd asked for a place in the sleeper car since the three of them had the farthest west to go. They went to the passenger car, fancy with padded seats and elegant wood paneling.

Accommodations sure had improved since he'd started helping place orphans. A sturdy water dispenser sat at the back of the car, now. Central heating made the journey far more bearable at night, too. The dust and wind from open windows during warmer weather hadn't changed, but every little bit of comfort otherwise helped. He and the twenty orphans he'd left Chicago with this week had ridden in luxury compared to the first five he'd wrangled seven years ago.

"Mr. Easton, can we sit together?" Mike asked.

Quincy scanned the car, finding an empty row at the very front of. Nearly everyone else had found their place by now. "Certainly. Go on up to the first seat."

Mike nodded and went on with Jake's hand in his.

Quincy followed them, frowning at the water trail they left. Hopefully, their pants weren't too wet, or he'd have to put them in their pajamas, also. They reached the padded bench with Jake sliding in first. Quincy smiled, glad Mike had remembered to let his shorter brother in first so both could see the passing country. "Take off your shoes and socks, boys, and put them under the seat to dry."

"Yes, sir," they said in unison as Quincy squished his carpetbag into the metal cage shelf above them.

Satisfied his luggage wouldn't fall, he sighed in relief. He hadn't brought anything breakable but didn't want the boys' belongings, in a sack within his bag, to be dented or smashed. Settling into his place beside Jake and Mike, he said, "Let's see the bottom of your pant legs." They lifted their feet, the hem soaked but not much else. The puddle had been shallow enough to not drench them. "Good. If you get cold, let me know, and I'll retrieve your pajamas."

Mike nodded before watching Jake stand on the seat to look out of the window. He slid over, leaning forward for a better view. Quincy smiled at the two. Not for the first time was he grateful the brothers got along so well. Some of the orphans hadn't, which made for tense times between him and the other agent Bran Gregory. He didn't mind too much disciplining the children when they acted up. Bran, on the other hand, didn't hesitate to apply corporal punishment as needed. Sometimes Quincy agreed, but most times, he figured children Mike and Jake's age just didn't know any better or forgot the rules.

Facing the front, Quincy stared at the newfangled lighting without really seeing it. He'd followed the Sisters' suggestion by keeping his voice soft with the children in case he ever needed to raise it for emphasis. Their advice worked. By the time he'd been to Kansas City, all the youngsters listened when he talked. Getting them to their new homes in Kansas and Missouri in good moods from being well behaved left him satisfied. Now, all he needed to do was get Jake and Mike to Sacramento and their new parents. Then, he'd go home to Chicago and do it all again with a different group of orphans needing placement with good people.

Mike's voice shook Quincy out of his reverie when he heard the boy ask, "What's your name? Are you a mother who needs a child of her own?"

He looked to find both Jake and Mike turned completely around. Mike stood on his knees while Jake was on his feet. Both faced the people behind him. He looked back and met the gaze of one of the most beautiful women he'd ever seen. Her eyes were the darkest green, framed by long lashes. The drab gray dress didn't detract from her rosy complexion, much, and her blonde hair had been tucked up under a narrow-brimmed hat to match her dress. He'd noticed many lovely women in his travels, but none took his breath like this young lady did. Twisting in his seat to see her better, he and the children eagerly waited for her answer.

She smiled at Quincy and answered Mike. "I'm Josie Simmons, and no, I'm not a mother yet. I'm on my way to meet my new husband and maybe have a family of my own someday." She gave Quincy a glance before refocusing on the two boys. "How about you?" She smiled at Quincy. "Are you and your brother on an adventure with your father?"

"No. We're going to our new parents," Mike answered. "Mr. Easton is placing us in our forever home."

"That's wonderful," she said and said to Quincy, "You're doing a beneficial service for children who need help, and that's commendable."

Such praise from a beautiful woman left him a little shy. He'd forgotten his hat days ago back home, or he'd tip the brim. Trying to keep his cheeks from overheating, he decided to brush aside her praise. "Thank you, and you can call me Quincy. Taking children to new homes is my work. I find it satisfying to know youngsters are finding families who'll love them."

"That's very important," Josie commented as the train shifted side to side, tossing Jake against the window.

Quincy heard the thump just before the boy started crying. He took the child in his arms, checking the bump on the child's head. "You're fine. Just a little tap," he tried to reassure him. Jake's only response was to cry louder. "Come on, then, it's nap time for both of you."

"I'm not sleepy," Mike argued as Quincy stood up with the younger boy in his arms.

"Of course not, but I'll need help with settling Jake down after we make the beds." He pulled their belongings from above them. "I'm counting on your help."

Mike's chest puffed out at being given responsibility. "I can carry the bag for you."

Quincy handed over their carpetbag then shifted Jake to his other hip. The boy nestled against him as if ready for sleep now. Giving a smile to their new acquaintance, Quincy said, "It was a pleasure meeting you, Miss Simmons. I hope we meet up again sometime."

"So do I," she said with a smile and went back to watching the landscape outside.

He took the hint to go on back to the sleeper car. They had to pass through a couple of passenger and dinner cars before getting to their beds. He found a place near the bathrooms before setting down Jake. "Do you need to visit the facilities before we rest a little?" Both boys nodded. "Very well." He took the bag from Mike, putting it on the seat. "I'll help." The train's side-to-side motion kept them from arguing as they single filed into the bathroom.

By the time Quincy had helped both boys potty and wash up, he was ready for a nap himself. Folding out the seats into beds took little time. Soon, both Jake and Mike were sleeping. He sighed in relief, glad to have a chance to take care of his own needs. He used the restroom, too, glad they'd upgraded to hand and face washing supplies.

Feeling better, he went to sit with the boys. He brushed the hair back from Mike's face. The young child talking to the young woman of his own accord was unusual. Ordinarily, Quincy would have to prod the youngster into using his words far more for manners' sake. Without the nudge, Mike would stand there quietly in front of anyone they'd met.

Quincy sank down in the seat, putting his feet up on the opposite side. He supposed any male, young or old, would take a liking to Josie. Now that the boys were settled, he could really reflect on her appearance without being rude. She seemed to smile easily, making her deep green eyes crinkle at the corners. Dark circles gave away how tiring her journey had been, and now? All he wanted to do was go back and ask why she was going to marry a man she'd never met.

He closed his eyes, letting his chin rest against his chest. She was probably one of those mail-order brides. Several young ladies from the orphanage chose their husbands after a few exchanged letters instead of hunting the city for a man. He couldn't blame them, considering the employment choices were few for a woman. Meanwhile, a single man could do anything from advertising shows at a circus to zigzagging across the country on cattle drives.

Given her mail-order bride probability, Quincy figured she might be as much of an orphan as he was. The more he thought about her, the more his need to go up front and talk to her grew unbearable. Except, he couldn't leave the sleeping children. If they woke up to find him gone, they'd be afraid. He sighed, regret filling him. She might be leaving the train at the next stop, and he'd never see her again.

Which didn't matter to him at all, he chided his conscience. Josie was practically married to someone else. None of his business. He leaned back, looking up at the ceiling. Just because she was the prettiest woman he'd ever seen and had given a warm smile to the boys didn't mean anything. He glanced over at the two. Mike had his arm around Jake as they slept, ever the protective big brother.

Except, if she did disembark at the next stop, Quincy would never have the answer to the questions he had about her. He stood. Five minutes away from them to wish Josie luck wouldn't hurt. The train wouldn't stop in the meantime. Besides, people took longer to visit the facilities than he planned to be gone. He pulled the curtains together to give the boys privacy before returning to Josie's train car.

Now faster alone than with the children, he moved down the narrow aisles, wobbly due to the train's motions. He passed through the train cars in a hurry. If he could reach Josie, say a few well wishes, and ask a few questions, he'd be back with the children in no time. Later, he'd think about why he needed to speak with her this last time.

As he entered her section, the seats beside and in front of Josie were empty. His heart started beating harder at his closeness to her. Even a train car apart, a sudden shyness took over, rooting him to the spot. What would he say to her? I think you're pretty and have a good life? No, he needed to be witty without being forward or silly.

"Excuse me, tickets, please."

Quincy dug in his pocket for the ticket, stepping aside so the conductor could enter the car entirely. "Yes, of course." He presented the document for the man to review.

"Good." He gave a quick nod. "Carry on and safe travels."

"Thank you." Wanting to get ahead of the man and before he lost his nerve, Quincy hurried down to the first seat. He sat, trying to act casual as he turned his back to the window. Josie rested her head on her hand, the elbow wedged on the window pane. Like the boys, she seemed to be napping as well as anyone could while sitting upright.

Too many people sat around them for him to have a chance to stare at her without causing comment.

A sudden shake startled Josie awake. When she opened her eyes and looked at him, Quincy felt as charmed as any snake in a basket ever had been. "Um, hello."

She frowned, putting a hand in front of her face while yawning. "What time is it? Have we been traveling long?" Before he could answer, she looked around them. "Where are Mike and Jake?"

How she'd remembered the boys' names warmed his heart. "We haven't even made our first stop yet, and they're taking an afternoon nap."

"Oh, good. I'd wanted to say goodbye and wish them well before they left." She smiled at him. "Although I'm sure with as much experience as you have with placing children, they don't need luck."

Quincy had a tough time remembering to keep their conversation short. "Thank you for thinking so highly of me. I'd come back to give you the same sentiments." Trying and failing to not pry, he asked, "You'd mentioned marrying a man you've never met. Anyone taking vows with a stranger needs all the best wishes they can get."

She blushed before looking down at her hands folded in her lap. "He's not too much of a stranger, though no, we've never met. We have happened to have exchanged several letters this past year."

He didn't know if he'd be able to marry a woman sight unseen. But then, desperate people did desperate things. At least they'd been able to connect via the mail. "Sounds like a good plan to learn more about each other."

"I agree. One of my friends married a man from a catalog with drawings of the men included. I've never seen anything but a small portrait of my fiancé." She stared out of the window as the train slowed. "He's rather handsome, but I suspect the personality in his letters helped my opinion of him."

Quincy mentally shrugged off the unnecessary envy filling him. Keeping his tone bright, he asked, "Do you have far to go before meeting your new husband?"

"I'm afraid so," Josie replied. She blushed a little before looking down at her gloved hands, folded in her lap. "I'm only three days into my trip from my aunt's home in Baltimore with four more to Sacramento."

She'd be with them until the boys reached their forever home? He almost felt like one of Sister Margaret's miracles had smacked him upside the head. "Well, what do you know. I'd been far too eager to say goodbye and wish you well. We're going to Sacramento, too. The boys' adoptive parents live there."

"You're taking two children all the way out to California? Are there no orphans to adopt out there?"

Before he could answer, Josie held up her hand. "No, I'm sorry. I'm far too nosy. It's really none of my business."

"There's nothing wrong with a healthy curiosity." He glanced at the back of the car. "If I weren't derelict in my duties, I'd sit and chat with you about my work at the Sisters of Mercy Orphanage."

Josie tilted her head to indicate the children sleeping in a car behind them. "You would, but you've left two young boys alone, supposedly napping, and heaven only knows the trouble they're getting into right now. Isn't that right?"

"Exactly."

She laughed, covering her mouth for a few seconds afterward. "I think you'd better check on them. If you want someone to keep them occupied while you need a break, just ask. You know where I'll be."

Quincy stood, only the boys' potential shenanigans motivating him to leave. She was an angel for offering, and he wanted to be sure she'd meant the kindness. "You won't mind?"

"Not at all. They're both adorable and charming."

He backed out of the seat. "I won't tell them you've said so, or they'll be your constant companions the entire way." Her smile warmed his heart, and he couldn't help but return her grin. "Will you join us for supper? Or are you looking forward to a quiet evening alone?"

Looking out of the window, she shook her head. "I'll

have to pass this time, but thank you for asking. Maybe later."

How her expression faded from happy to tense bothered Quincy, but he ignored the nagging feeling for now. "Very well, miss. Have a good night."

"You too," she replied before he left.

CHAPTER 2

Josie stood, stretching her stiff muscles. The Omaha train station wasn't far behind them, yet the ride from Baltimore was beginning to take its toll. At least the seats were comfortably padded. Scooting over to the aisle, she removed her carpetbag from the overhead storage. She didn't expect anyone to run off with her belongings, of course. Not on an enclosed train. Still, maybe Aunt Erma was right. People might be kind, but not all of them could be trusted.

She went to the back of the car to where the water cooler sat. The dense ceramic container stayed full enough to be steady, no matter how rough the track became. She wiped the community cup with her sleeve. Not because she was prissy like her aunt often called her, but because the idea of some other passenger's drool was too much to bear at the moment. Refreshed, she took a bathroom break before going back to her seat.

The scenery passing by went on for what seemed like an eternity. The ride between Chicago and Omaha hadn't appeared to have featured such wide-open spaces. She smiled, digging into the bag beside her without bothering to look. A train ride at night did keep the sightseeing down to almost nothing. A lack of a full moon didn't help, either. With a book on her lap and an apple wrapped in a napkin in her hand, she began eating.

Meeting the two young boys had been delightful, talking with their guardian even more so. Quincy looked more like a big brother or even father figure than an adoption agency's representative. Josie took another bite. Although, how would she know? Aunt Erma had kept her out of the orphanage when her parents had died. As bad as the tales her aunt had threatened her with had been, Mike and Jake seemed much more cared for.

Surprised to bite into an apple core, Josie looked to find nothing meaty on the apple remained. If she tried, there were a couple of nibbles left at either end. She twisted the stem once for each letter while saying the alphabet. Fully expecting to reach "W" for Wilbert, the stem snapped off at "Q." She pecked the last bit of edible apple, knowing full well what Aunt Erma would say about superstition. Quincy was on her mind, and that's all. A tiny unconscious tug on an apple stem didn't mean anything. Finished, she wrapped up her waste for later disposal. Even a few cars behind her, the dining car's aroma let her know the staff was starting supper.

Josie sighed. This trip couldn't be over soon enough. She didn't feel safe, wouldn't, until firmly wedded to her unmet groom. Lowering the window a bit, she peeked out despite the rush of wind as they traveled. Nothing but flat up ahead. Wild, lovely, but barren enough to continue reading *An Old-Fashioned Girl*. She cracked open her book, and soon, she was lost in the story.

"Hey, Miss Josie."

Mike's precious voice pulled her from her book's drama. He stood at the end of her seat with Jake beside him. She smiled at the towheaded boys, placing a bookmark in before shoving the novel and napkin back into her bag. "Hello, Mike, Jake. How was your supper?"

"The best." Mike didn't wait for an invitation, hopping up onto the seat next to her. Jake did the same as his brother continued, "Mr. Easton let us have dessert."

Sweets? Only now did she grow jealous. Still, she understood why Quincy couldn't deny them a treat. "Really? What did you have?"

"Apple pie with whipped cream. We had roast beef and potatoes, too." He began swinging his feet. "Mr. Easton also said we could go outside to play at the next stop."

"There you two are."

She turned at the familiar voice to see Quincy approaching them. His dark hair stood up on end as if he'd been running his hands through the strands. His deep brown eyes twinkled when their gazes met. Smiling at him, she asked, "You didn't know they were here?"

"I had a suspicion after listening to them talk about you all through dinner." Quincy came over and sat in front of the trio, his back against the window to face her. "Neither boy wanted us to start eating without you."

Josie raised an eyebrow at the boys, who then nodded. She reached over and ruffled Mike's hair. "That's very kind, but there's never a need to wait for me. I had my supper already."

Quincy frowned. "You did? In here?"

"Yes, a very satisfying one." She crossed her fingers ever so slightly for the necessary fib. "Between the train's motion and how crowded the dining car can be, I like keeping my meals small."

"Makes sense," he said. "Still, sometime when you're feeling better, you're welcome to join us."

"I'll keep that in mind." She glanced outside, the bright orange thundercloud catching her attention in the late evening glow. "I'd hoped for one last stop before nightfall."

Before she could say anything more, Mike tugged her sleeve. "We're going to meet our new parents. Do you have parents? Ours will be forever if we're good. I have to help Jake sometimes, so he'll stay with me and not be sent to a different home."

She gave Quincy a sharp glance, a bit ill and not from the constant sway from the tracks. "Even bad boys have homes forever. Or they should." She faced Mike again. "I'm sure, despite your worst conduct, you're still very good and have nothing to worry about."

Quincy cleared his throat, getting her attention. "Both children are extremely well behaved. The Morgans will be fortunate in adopting Jake and Mike. Also, the Sisters of Mercy insist siblings stay together no matter what."

"I'm glad you think so," she said. The train began slowing. She smiled at the boys, saying, "I think we're stopping soon. Didn't you mention something about playing outside?"

"We did," Mike replied and hopped off of the seat with Jake following him.

Moving fast to stop their escape, Quincy slid down the chair, ready to block their way. "Oh no, you don't. Stay with me until the train is completely stopped." The boy gave him a devilish grin and took another step. Quincy frowned at him. "Keep going, then, and see what you get."

Laughing at how adorably mischievous the child behaved would do Quincy no good. She stared straight ahead, biting her lip to keep from chuckling out loud.

When the brakes squealed as the train shuddered to a stop, Quincy stood in the aisle. "Now we can go," he said, and the boys took off, weaving among the other passengers in the corridor. "Stay on the platform, and don't leave sight of the depot." His voice grew louder the farther the children ran away from them. Josie allowed a laugh when he shook his head. He grinned at her. "Usually, those two never talk to strangers. After they peppered you with questions today, I might need to start warning them."

Being special to someone, even if they were only children, warmed Josie's heart. "I don't mind. Talking with them helps break up the tedium."

"Speaking of excitement, would you like to see the depot with us? It's not too thrilling, I'm sure, but I could use some fresh air."

"So could I." The car cleared a little more, so Josie stood up, ready to take a chance and walk outside for a little while. She retrieved her traveling bag while he waited. As soon as she was in the aisle, he went on, clearing the way for her to follow. She stepped out onto the platform after him, the wind lifting her bonnet a little. "Goodness!" escaped her. "I didn't expect this even after the train stopped.

Quincy laughed. "Yeah, the plains takes some getting used to. No trees around to block the wind." He started for the depot building. "I think this station has fresh coffee."

His familiarity with the stop surprised Josie. She went

along with him, noting how he checked on Mike and Jake playing tag on the platform. "Have you been here before?"

"A few times." He held the door open for her. "I've brought children to homes in western Nebraska, but not much farther." Other passengers' conversations echoed in the large room, leading him to speak up a bit. "I'm eager to see what's on the other side of the state's border."

The warm smell of coffee greeted Josie when he poured her a cup. Taking the offered drink from him, she said, "I am, too. I've heard we'll go through mountains higher than any most people will ever see."

"Snowcapped, even now, I reckon." He took a sip. "We should probably keep an eye on the boys."

Josie followed him to one of the large windows near the door. "If they're anything like I was as a child, they're already in trouble."

Mike was crawling around, giving Jake a ride on his back. Quincy shook his head. "I suppose they needed a good scrubbing anyway. They'll get a wipe down tonight and a solid dunking when we reach Sacramento."

"I like that idea for all of us," she said.

He laughed. "I won't take that as a hint for me and my hygiene as much as wishful thinking for you."

She took a sip, trying to not grin. "You might be right."

"I can see why you mentioned being a wild child."

His smile told her he couldn't be serious. She drank the

last of her coffee, holding her hand out for his empty cup. "The line back on board is already forming."

He took a last drink before letting her have his empty container. "Thank you, since it always takes a bit of convincing to get them back in a seat."

"I can imagine," she said as he left. Watching him scoop up Jake first, then Mike like they were five-pound flour bags, she enjoyed how he interacted with the children. His handsome face might have gained her interest, but his kindness kept her attention. Almost ready to stop staring and put the cups away, she noticed him look back at the depot. The expression on his face stopped her heart for a second. His longing struck a chord within her. She shared the same loneliness despite the letters from Wilbert.

Wilbert. Darn and double darn. With a shake, she turned to put their cups on a dirty dish tray. She needed to remember her groom. Wilbert was who waited patiently at the end of the journey for her hand in marriage, not Quincy. She left the depot, the cold air chilling her in a way she felt she deserved. Quincy might be kind and handsome, but he wasn't her intended at all. She stepped onto the train as the final all aboard whistle sounded before making her way to her usual seat.

Quincy and the boys were nowhere to be found. Josie put away her bag and sat, glad they weren't there after all. Not that she didn't adore the children because who wouldn't? It was their guardian. She had met him hours ago, yet he'd led her to almost forgetting her engagement. She stared out at the nearly dark land as the train started pulling out of the station. Four days on a train, and she'd be in Sacramento. She'd waited a lifetime for her distant husband, so surely she could stay focused on Wilbert until they met.

Feeling a tug on her sleeve, Josie turned from the vista to find Mike seated beside her with Jake beside him. The oldest boy grinned, his missing tooth clearly showing. "Come to bed with us. We want to hear a story."

Josie was tempted to give in to his request, except she didn't know their guardian's plans for the evening. Mike could be trying to extend his bedtime just as she often had at his age. "I'm sure Mr. Easton has plenty of stories to tell you."

"We've heard all of his," Mike replied, leaning against her.

Jake nodded and put his arms around her leg. "We want you."

"I see." She glanced over at a movement to her side. Quincy leaned against the empty seat behind her with a wry grin. "If Mr. Easton approves, I suppose I could tell you about Polly's new city friends."

"Josie will be in a different sleeper car and too busy tonight," Quincy said. "Won't you be?"

She smiled, reaching over to pat Jake on the back. She ignored the remorse over not getting to spend time with the boys, saying, "Something like that, yes."

The boys stared at him with the most woebegone eyes Josie had ever seen. Before she could ask Quincy to change his mind for their sakes, he said, "Still, I guess one story won't hurt, if you have the time."

She grinned and made a go along motion with her hand. "You heard him. First, let's get you both cleaned up and in pajamas, ready to hear adventures."

The duo cheered and ran for the back of the car, not waiting for either adult. As Josie left her seat, Quincy asked, "Do you have a place to rest tonight?" A couple of nearby passengers snickered, and his face flushed a bright red. "I mean, I didn't mean anything. Just, the sleeper cars seem rather full already, that's all."

She glared at the amused men before replying, "I'm fine, really. I'd planned on skipping the extra cost of a bunk for this trip."

"For how long?" he asked, following her to the back and through the door. "You've been on the train four days already."

Waiting until he opened the door for her, she said, "No, three so far and four more to go. I'll admit, I'm a little tired, but tonight means I'm halfway finished."

"Seven days with nearly no rest?" He led her through the second passenger car and to the crowded dinner car. "No, I can't let any woman go so long without sleep. At least now I know why you have dark circles under your eyes."

His comment stung both in a place it should and somewhere it shouldn't. Josie wanted to look lovely for Wilbert, yet she already cared far too much what Quincy thought of her. She couldn't help but ask, "They're not so bad, are they?"

He paused at the last door to look at her. "No, you're still beautiful, if not dead on your feet."

"Oh." He did have a point. Exhaustion fogged her mind, and the days were starting to run together. "Thank you, but I'm not all that tired."

Quincy didn't open the sleeper car's door. Instead, he faced her with his hand on the latch. "You'll sleep in my bed tonight, without me, of course, and I can't take no for an answer."

Being told what to do after having several days of freedom from Aunt Erma's barked orders rankled her. Josie shook her head even as she trailed behind him into the sleeper car. "In this case, you will let me do as I please. I'm not one of your orphans, plus, I won't take something I didn't pay for."

He was quiet for a moment next to the boys' bunk

before saying, "Very well. I won't ask again, but I would like a favor."

She stepped aside, as did he, to let someone pass through to his sleeping place. Once somewhat alone again, she said, "All right, I can grant a kindness depending on what it is."

"Could you mind the boys while I clean up?" He interlaced his fingers together as if praying. "You could sit and have a little wait. Maybe get comfortable. I promise I won't take long. Plus, you'd have my undying gratitude for keeping watch over them."

CHAPTER 3

"Mr. Easton," a female voice hissed before someone shook him. "Mr. Easton, wake up this instant."

"Hmm?" Quincy opened his eyes to find Josie standing at the end of his seat in the passenger car. He sat up from a slouch, rubbing his eyes. "What if I don't want to?"

"You will, and you will go back to the boys." She slid into the empty seat next to him. "I can't believe you'd lie to me like you have. Pretending you needed a toilet visit only to sneak back here."

He took in how her color seemed better. No more dark smudges marred the skin under her eyes. Despite her clucking, Josie had needed a solid night's rest, even if it was in his bunk. "It was the only way I could get you to sleep in a comfortable place."

"You need to apologize this instant for making me sleep

in your bunk," she hissed. "What if someone on here knows Wilbert and tells him I was in a strange man's bed?"

Quincy couldn't help but chuckle. "First of all, I wasn't there, so your being in my bunk doesn't matter one bit."

"It's all about appearances, Mr. Easton." She folded her hands on her lap. "I look loose, coming from a sleeping car like I did just now."

He leaned closer to her to speak quietly. "Are you telling me all of the ladies on their way to breakfast now are considered loose women?" He wagged his eyebrows for emphasis. "Because if so, I sure hope they like young men from Chicago."

She fumed, saying, "You. Are. Horrible," and giving his arm a slap with an unfilled glove with each word. "I suppose I'm lucky you let me sleep there at all, considering how proper I am."

Her words reminded him of how she'd not been well-rested until last night, and maybe not even then. Sobering up real quick, he said, "Not lucky, but you just had someone who knows what it's like to want a warm bed to sleep in. I can always take a nap with the boys this afternoon." He lowered his voice so only the two of them could hear him. "That way, you'll get some rest tonight when you retake my bunk."

She leaned away from him. "Oh, no. I'm a little outraged but more upset you didn't have the bed you'd paid for. I'll be fine. The trip might be grueling while I'm traveling, but once I'm with Wilbert? I'll get plenty of sleep."

He hooked his thumbs in his pockets and stared ahead, trying to not smile. "I wouldn't venture to say anything about how much a person sleeps on their honeymoon, Miss Simmons." He chuckled at her outraged gasp. "See? I'm right about you keeping watch over the children. You needed the rest."

"No, surely..." She cleared her throat. "No, I'll be fine traveling as I was until Omaha. I didn't pay for a sleeper, and you did."

Technically, the orphanage paid. Quincy was about to tell Josie so when the thought occurred to him. "Are you an orphan, too? Or did you merely live with your aunt to care for her?"

Josie shrugged. "I don't consider myself an orphan. My parents died when I was fourteen. Almost old enough to marry, if I were willing to take the first man who asked."

His heart fell to his stomach. Sure, some girls married early, but fourteen? The young ladies at the Sisters of Mercy seemed far too young to vow the rest of their life to a man. "You were proposed to at such a tender age?"

She gave him a wry grin, turning a little in the seat to face him. "Yes, one of my father's friends offered for my hand at the funeral. I thought he meant to marry his son, so I accepted at first."

"Good Lord." A man the age of Josie's father taking her as a wife sickened Quincy. "You didn't go through with the ceremony, did you?"

"Oh no, not at all." She leaned a little closer to him. "As soon as I found out who he meant for me to marry, I refused. My aunt took me in, begrudgingly, but kept me safe nonetheless."

"I'm glad you rejected him," Quincy said before thinking. A slight smile played around her lips as he stammered, "I mean, a person should marry for love, not out of desperation."

"You're a lucky man who can say so." She stood to let him out into the aisle. "Not everyone can be in love when they marry."

"Like you?" he asked, sliding over to join her in standing. "I mean, you can't have true feelings for him, can you?" As soon as he saw the mutinous expression on her face, he tried to backtrack. "Forgive me, I've spoken out of turn. Of course, you have feelings for…"

"Wilbert," she offered and turned to the back of the train.

Quincy followed, saying, "Right. Wilbert. Otherwise, you'd not be on your way to marry him."

She paused at the first junction between the passenger cars for a moment. "Exactly so."

He kept going, keeping up as she hurried farther back. "Where are we going?"

"To Mike and Jake before they wake up missing you."

"Oh, horsefeathers!" he said as visions of the two wreaking havoc along the train came to mind. He'd been so caught up in talking with Josie, the two boys never came to mind. "I appreciate you coming to get me, Miss Simmons."

"My pleasure, and thank you for letting me sleep."

He gave her a nod, and when she hesitated at the last exit, he continued on, leaving the car. Irritated for letting himself get sidetracked by a pretty girl, Quincy hurried to the boys. The closer he came to where their bunk, the more he hoped they still slept. When he reached their sleeping berth, he pulled the curtain back a bit and relaxed. The boys were sound asleep. He thanked whatever saint might be his helper.

The train eased to a stop. The constant noise of being in motion ended, too, making it far easier to hear snores and conversation. No one walked through the sleeper car, which made having privacy far easier.

Not feeling rested, due to sleeping while sitting upright, Quincy kicked off his shoes. He sat on the bed beside Mike and found a seat back to lean against. Slumping down to recline as much as possible, he resisted the urge to give in and lie down under the covers. Breakfast would be in a couple of hours. He had plenty of time to relax and think about Josie.

Quincy lay there for goodness knows how long, picking apart every word they'd said to each other. Josie's every shy glance out of the window. The way she hid her smiles behind her hand. He loved how her eyes sparkled when the two of them talked about Jake and Mike. Whoever had placed the ad for a bride was a fortunate man. He just hoped the guy knew the prize he'd marry.

"Mr. Easton. Jake needs to go potty."

Mike shook Quincy's body, his urgent tone waking him from a sound sleep. Jake's knee digging into his manly bits as he climbed over also brought him into sitting upright. "Hey, no need to go anywhere without me." He scooped the boy up and over onto the floor. Food aromas hit the three of them full-on when he opened the curtain. Anticipating the next question, he answered, "Yes, we'll go for breakfast after Jake's finished in the restroom."

"Me, too," Mike said.

"Me three," Quincy agreed, opening the door and ushering Jake inside first. The Sisters had made the children's clothes easy to put on and take off for the smaller children. Improvising better methods led to a lot of time-saving, appreciated when he needed to care for more than four children at a time. He leaned against the door, "Be sure to wash your hands when finished, Jake. We'll want to go eat when we're all finished."

A small and muffled, "Yes, Mr. Easton," sounded through the wood panel.

Quincy enjoyed having fewer charges to herd to new homes. The other agent with him, Bran, went back to Chicago after the last orphan had been spoken for. He sighed. If not for a childless couple wanting children, he'd be on his way home as well. And then? He would never have met Josie. Jake's emergence from the washroom distracted him. "All right, next?" he said to Mike.

The older boy took his turn, leaving Quincy free to resume his musing about Josie. Something deeper had to be going on in her life, more than just wanting a husband. Didn't most women marry a man from church or their childhood sweetheart? He'd never been tempted to wonder how a lady picked her husband until now.

Mike finishing his toiletry gave Quincy a chance to take care of his business. Once done, he stepped out to find the boys waiting for him. He smiled, glad these two were well behaved. "Are you hungry?"

"Starving," Mike replied. "Feels like we haven't eaten for days."

Quincy laughed at the youngster's melodrama. "The dinner car smells that good, huh?" The boy nodded as Quincy took his and Jake's hands. "Then let's go before we all waste away." He led them to the dining car. Just as they settled in with the boys wearing napkins tucked into their collars, Josie walked into the room. He gave her a wave. She didn't respond even though he was sure she'd noticed the three of them. "I'll be right back. Think about what you want to eat, and we'll order when I return."

He walked up to Josie as she waited by the door. "Hello. Haven't I seen you around here before?" he quipped.

She smiled. "Not here, but nearby for sure." After giving a quick nod to the boys, she returned her attention to him. "The children look too clean to have had eaten yet."

"You noticed?" He chuckled. "We haven't ordered anything." Acting as if the thought suddenly occurred to him, he asked, "Won't you join us? I know the children would love your company."

"I can't. I'm sorry. You are all wonderful company, but I really need to get back to my seat." She didn't meet his eyes but motioned to a server at the other end of the car. "I'm here for a takeaway breakfast." Before Quincy could say anything else, she stepped up to the young man. "Hello, I'd like either an apple or biscuit, please. Whichever is the least cost."

"It'll be the biscuit. I can bring jam and butter to you if you'd have a seat here."

She waved a hand as if to ward him off. "No, thank you. I need to hurry back."

"Yes, ma'am."

Quincy watched him walk to the exit, slipping into the cooking area. "You're not having much to eat."

Josie shrugged as if a tiny meal was an ordinary occurrence. "I don't need a lot, and besides, I need to be frugal until Sacramento. I'm on a tight budget, and anything might happen."

Her carefree attitude about sleeping upright and now having a biscuit as a full breakfast worried him. "So much so that a bunk and decent meals cost too much?"

Josie's smile wavered. "I'm afraid so."

So her frugality wasn't by choice. Before Quincy could say anything else, the young server returned. He barely listened to the man and Josie's conversation. His distraction from being worried kept him from paying attention to anything else but his irritation. When the server was gone, he asked, "Did your groom not send enough to ensure comfortable travel?"

She frowned. "Wilbert didn't need to. I've saved my pin money for a year, and it's been enough if I budget appropriately."

Quincy couldn't look at her directly, or she'd see the rage he felt for her fiancé burning there. How dare a man ask for a woman to travel across the country, but not send her enough funds to be safe? Anything could happen between Baltimore and Sacramento. Josie could be stranded anywhere in between with nothing for a place to sleep. Even worse, she'd been sleeping upright and subsisting on whatever the least expensive item on the menu was. Before he could talk himself out of the idea, he offered, "Why not join us for breakfast? The boys never eat everything they're given."

"I couldn't."

"You could because I'm taking care of the rest, and my pants are getting too small for me." He tucked a thumb into his waistband for extra emphasis. "See? You'd be doing me a favor."

"I'd better go and find my seat," she said as the train lurched to a stop. "Otherwise, someone else will sit there."

"No other place will do?" he asked, puzzled by her doggedness to be in the same spot every day.

"I know I'm particular. Would you like me to fetch your overnight bag from the bunk?" She held up her own. "The people seem well-behaved on here, but it only takes one person with bad intentions."

"Thank you, I'd appreciate the gesture."

Josie nodded. "Very well, I'll stop to get it, and you'll know where to find me when you're finished."

He'd rather find her with him instead of sleeping in a passenger car. "You're not getting off to stretch your legs?"

"No, not until the afternoon." She smiled at the boys, interrupting their playing with Quincy's red bandanna by saying, "I'll see you both later."

The boys waved, and Quincy sat a little taller. His manners lessons had been somewhat practical. If he could just get them to use a fork, they'd be almost ready for their new parents.

CHAPTER 4

Josie watched as the train entered the Sacramento city limits an hour earlier than the timetables had indicated. She'd done it, avoided Quincy, Mike, and Jake for the past few days despite their best efforts. After the first breakfast, when the boys brought her a boxed meal, she knew nothing less than finding another section of the train would do. She'd accepted their gift before finding a seat in a passenger car near the caboose.

Why?

Because of Quincy. She chewed the last little bit of thumbnail, only quitting when tasting blood yet again. He looked at her the way a man should when he loves a woman. All soft-eyed, ready to smile in an instant as if he can't help himself. She sighed, putting her thumb inside her closed fist to stop the slight bleeding. Wilbert was who she'd promised her life to, not the handsome adoption agent. She forgot her fiancé every time Quincy was near. The boys didn't help, either. Jake and Mike made seeing the agent as a father far too easy.

She shifted in her seat, ready to disembark the slowing train. Grab her luggage, leave, find Quin—no, Wilbert, she scolded. She needed to find her almost-husband without meeting up with anyone else. No wishful thoughts and dreams, no fantasies about life as an agent's wife, and certainly no imagining kisses from anyone except her dear Wilbert. She'd reread his letters to her several times in the past two days as a reminder. Sitting up straighter, she ignored the urge to leap into the aisle and run to find Quincy.

The chilly fresh air hit her as soon as she stepped onto the platform. Somewhat dazed, she blinked in the bright spring sunshine. More massive than she expected, the city stretched out in all directions. The buildings were so much newer than anything she'd seen in Baltimore, and shorter, too.

"Miss?"

She turned to see a porter, but before she could say anything, he added, "Do you have any other bags to claim?"

"No, thank you," Josie replied. He went to the next passenger, and she quickened her pace. Her grip tightened on the worn leather handle she held. Maybe by hurrying, she'd be with Wilbert before Quincy and the boys realized she'd gone.

Mike yelled, "Miss Simmons!" before plowing into her, soon followed by Jake. "We're so glad you didn't leave us after all."

Quincy approached her and the boys from across the platform. "You two, come on. Your new parents will be here any moment." He nodded at Josie, "Miss Simmons, a pleasure."

His grim expression didn't match his cheerful words. Still, Josie wanted to try to coax one last smile out of Quincy. Face to face like this, she didn't want to part ways with him thinking less of her. "Likewise, Mr. Easton. Meeting you and the children were the high points of my journey."

The sternness seeped from his face, softening his frown. "I'm glad. We enjoyed your company for a while, too."

"Yes, for a little while." She held onto the bag with both hands. "I felt a bit distracted by my affections for the children. I didn't want them hurt when I had to leave *them* for Wilbert."

Quincy searched around them. "Speaking of, since he's not here, would you mind helping me wrangle the children into something presentable for the Morgans when they arrive?"

He hadn't caught her hint that she needed to focus on

Wilbert instead of dreaming about him, then. She faked a smile, knowing they'd be apart forever soon enough. "Certainly. I'd love to."

"Great." He let out a whistle. "Mike, Jake, let's clean up." The two came running over to them. Quincy took Mike's hand while Jake reached for Josie's.

She let go of her carpetbag to hold his small fingers with hers. He gave a little hop with every step as she said, "You're not too dirty. A little hand washing and hair combing, and you'll be fine." Quincy led the way to the washrooms, almost at the men's room door when she hesitated, asking, "Do you think anyone would mind if Jacob came with me?"

He thought a second before opening the men's room door. "I don't see how they would unless they're already using the facilities."

Josie took his advice and led Jake into the room. She kept the door unlocked behind her in case some woman needed a toilet. Smiling at the boy before digging around in her bag for a mostly clean napkin, she asked, "Are you excited to meet your new parents?"

"Um-hmm," he replied as she dipped a corner of the cloth into a pitcher of water. "They're taking us to a forever home, Mike said."

"That's right." She wiped his face to be sure, even though he seemed clean, before focusing on his hands. "I'm sure Mr. Easton has made certain they're the best parents possible for you and your brother."

"Uh-huh. He took care of us."

It took her a few seconds to understand him due to his grimacing during her scrubbing between his fingers. She smiled, searching her bag for a brush. "Now then, we need to detangle your hair." The boar bristles might be harsh on his tender scalp, so she gently combed his blond hair into a side part. Satisfied, she leaned back to give him one final inspection. He stared back at her with such solemn blue eyes she couldn't help but smile. "There. Very handsome."

"You're pretty. Mr. Easton says so."

"Oh?" While she'd love to know how Jake managed to hear such a thing from Quincy, a lady opened the door. Josie stood straight. "Hello, we're just leaving."

"Thank you. Train rides upset my stomach something fierce."

Not needing another hint, Josie threw her brush and napkin into her bag before leading Jake out into the hallway. Quincy and Mike were nowhere nearby, so she tapped on the men's room door. "Mr. Easton?"

"Yeah? We're still getting ready." The door opened, and Quincy peeked out. "Would you have a comb? I seem to have misplaced mine."

"I have a brush." She handed it over to him.

He grinned. "Thank you. We're almost done. Wait for us here?"

"Certainly," she replied before thinking about what Wilbert would prefer. "Oh, wait, Quincy, I can't. I need to see if my fiancé is here yet." In all of the excitement in cleaning up Jake, she'd completely forgotten about her soon to be husband. "Can I leave Jake with you and check?"

Quincy's face appeared again. "Yes, but feel free to come back if you'd like. We could keep you company until the Morgans arrive."

His face seemed so hopeful that she couldn't help but nod. "I'll check and be back soon if he isn't here yet." Hurrying away before he could respond, she searched the lobby for any man matching Wilbert's description. No one was tall enough, young enough, or even friendly enough. With a lingering glance toward the restrooms, she hurried out onto the train platform. No one stood there as the locomotive began moving on to the last western station. She turned to go find Quincy and the boys until remembering the Morgans. A few couples milled around. Some already had children, while others certainly must have grandchildren.

Josie bit her lip. It wouldn't be fair to anyone if she didn't let Quincy know the adoptive parents were possibly in the lobby. She went to the restrooms as the three exited.

"Wilbert isn't here yet, but the boys' mother and father might be.

"Already? All right." He knelt. "You two find a bench to sit and stay neat on. I need to chat with Miss Josie for a moment. Can you behave for a short while?"

"Yes, sir. We're not babies," Mike replied.

Jake nodded. "Not babies."

Josie would beg to differ but kept quiet as Quincy stood. "Very well. Wait for me inside the station. Neither of you is to go outside at all, and I'll be along soon." When both children were out of earshot, he turned to her. "I know this is impetuous, and I shouldn't let them out of my sight, but I need to talk with you."

Her heart began skipping beats at his serious and intense demeanor. She gripped her bag's handle tighter. "All right, what can I help you with?"

He opened a skinny door between the two restrooms and pulled her into the small closet. A small window above the threshold let scant light into the dim room. "Josie, I know this is too forward, but have you considered not meeting Wilbert? Considered going back to Chicago with me?"

She'd be lying if she said no, she'd never imagined skipping her mail-order engagement. "I...I've tried to not think about you instead of him."

"But?"

"But I've met you, know what a kind person you are, and how very attractive." Her last words left her as a whisper.

Quincy put his arms around her. "I'd have to be handsome to attract a beauty like you." He leaned in, brushing his lips against hers. "My heart has been yours since we met, Josie."

He kissed her with more ardor, his passion creating a fire in her she couldn't ignore any longer. Josie returned his desire with her arms around his neck to hold him close. He felt right, his lean hard body pressed against her softer one. She hadn't been so content, excited, and safe all at once, ever. Not even when Wilbert's letters arrived—

Like a locomotive's metal wheels grinding against the iron train tracks, her mind screeched to a halt. She stopped kissing Quincy. "Mr. Easton, this is, well, it's inappropriate, and we need to check on the boys."

He let go of her gently, as if forcing himself to step back. "You're right. I took liberties I had no right to."

"You did, but my complaint doesn't lie there." She took a deep breath and blurted, "I had to stay away from you, or our kiss would have happened far sooner. Now that our curiosity is satisfied, we can continue on with life."

"I see." He opened the door. "And you're right. I'll leave first, and you may leave a little later to avoid gossip since you're a new resident of the city."

A sick fear gripped her stomach. Wilbert could be waiting for her, sitting next to the boys, and she'd leave the broom closet with Quincy. "Very good, and thank you for thinking of me."

Quincy kissed her cheek, said, "I always do," before going.

She counted to thirty before easing her way out of the closet. Entering the main lobby area, Quincy faced her. He stood before a man and woman. Mike held the man's hand while Jake was sitting on the woman's hip. This must be the adoptive parents, then. She ignored how her nose stung from the threatening tears. Hoping to avoid a scene, she turned for the exit toward the station's platform. The large clock on the wall showed their posted arrival time was close. Wilbert should be here any minute.

Josie went farther out onto the wooden deck. Since their train had left the station already, and no one else waited there. A brisk wind stirred dust. She shivered, deciding watching for Wilbert through the depot's glass windows couldn't hurt. Once in the warmer building, she'd been inside just in time to see Quincy, the Morgans, and the boys leave through the front door. When Quincy glanced back at her, she gave him a little wave. His smile didn't reach his eyes as he followed the quartet out of the building.

She sighed and stared down at the ground for a few

seconds. Quincy was gone, then. If more families around Sacramento adopted, she might see him again. A very long shot and highly unlikely considering Wilbert's distant farm. Impatient to meet her betrothed, she went to the front windows and looked out. Every time a man with the barest resemblance to what she thought Wilbert might look like passed by, she stood a little straighter, ready to wave at him.

"Miss, the next train is tomorrow morning. Were you supposed to be met here?"

Tearing her gaze from outside and focusing on the stationmaster, she nodded. "Yes, my fiancé will be here soon. He's coming into town, and I'm sure he's just delayed a little." An idea hit her, so she asked, "You might know him. Have you heard of Wilbert Peppers?"

The man thought for a moment before answering, "No, I'm afraid not. The train heading east will be here in a few hours. I'll have to close up afterward."

"All right. I'm sure my fiancé will be here before then," Josie replied, suddenly worried she might be lying to him and herself.

CHAPTER 5

Every step Quincy took seemed harder than the one before. Mike was telling Mr. Morgan all about the train ride. Jake snuggled into Mrs. Morgan's arms. He followed the new family to one of the finest wagons he'd seen this side of the Missouri River. The boys would live an extraordinary life with the Morgans, he was sure of it.

"Mr. Easton," Chuck began. "Would you like to visit the farm? Be our guest for a few days?"

"Come on, dearest," Nancy began. "You saw the pretty girl standing nearby. He probably wants to go back and chase her down for a talk."

"I do need to see the boys' new home," Quincy admitted but stopped short of confessing his wish to return to the depot. Just because he needed to find Josie, that didn't mean he also needed to own up to the Morgans.

Chuck put a hand on Quincy's back, and said, "Tell you what. Come out to the house with us, have some lunch, then I'll drive you back here."

"Two trips to town in one day seems like a lot of trouble for you. I don't want to be a bother."

"You brought our boys to us," Nancy said.

Her husband put an arm around his wife. "How about I rent a horse for you?"

Mike and Jake stared at Quincy with pleading eyes to agree, convincing him. "Very well, but only if *I* can rent the horse."

Grinning from ear to ear, Chuck offered, "No, let me hire your ride for you. It's the least I can do for you keeping our boys safe."

"There's no need. I can use the allowance from the agency." Sensing an argument brewing from the set of Chuck's jaws, Quincy continued, "They expect me to visit the children's home on this trip since it's our first so far west."

"Then follow us once you're in the saddle." Chuck reached out his hand for Quincy to shake. "It'll be a pleasure showing you our setup."

Quincy gave him a nod before hurrying to the nearby livery. Soon, he'd rented a decent animal, mounting the horse as soon as the stable boy brought him to the front.

The Morgans, which included Mike and Jake now, sat in the wagon waiting for him. Quincy trotted over to them. "Are we ready? No errands to run before leaving town?"

"Hyah," Chuck replied, snapping the reins. The wagon began rolling. "No. We bought our supplies earlier this week."

Nancy leaned forward to see around her husband. "I wanted our home to be perfect for the boys."

"Will we have toys?" Mike asked from his perch next to Nancy.

"Yes," she replied. "You're almost old enough for your own pony."

"Pony?" Jake asked. "I want a pony."

His new father put an arm around the small boy next to him. "I have one for you, son. It's not real yet, but when you're old enough, too, you'll have a true horse of your own."

Something close to envy snaked its way through Quincy. The Morgans continued to talk about the boys' new home, but he stopped listening. The Sisters back at the orphanage did what they could for him, but to have a horse of his own? No one with his background could ever dream so big. Orphaned children all across the States would have lives far better than his and the other boys who grew up in the system. His gaze met Jake's. The youngster wore a smile and swung his feet under the wagon bench. Happiness for the siblings replaced envy in a second. He had missed out on parents but could ensure every other child had a real home.

Lost in his musing, Quincy realized how once out of town, the road narrowed in places. The one bridge they'd passed over had been a single lane from what he could recall. He rode beside the wagon, dropping back to allow oncoming vehicles the needed space. So far, he'd been able to keep his mind on the new family. And, thinking of families, he wondered what Josie was doing right now. Was she saying her wedding vows in front of a minister or judge? Had she stepped foot into her new home, or did Wilbert live far outside of town? He'd been more focused on learning more about her during their trip than about her unmet fiancé. Now he wished he'd asked more about her plans.

What he wanted to learn didn't matter. Josie had a new husband by now or at least soon enough for him to stop thinking about her. He resisted the urge to look back at the flat land behind them. Instead, he focused on the gentle hills and clusters of trees in front of them. By this time next week, he'd be in Chicago and ready to help another group of children find their forever homes. He wouldn't even remember Josie's name.

"She was really nice. She told stories at nap time," Mike told Nancy. "We shared our breakfast with her."

Jake added, "She cleaned my hands."

"She did?" Chuck said. Facing Quincy, he asked, "Did you bring one of the Sisters with you? She was welcome to come along to our farm."

Shaking his head, Quincy admitted, "Miss Simmons was just a friend we'd made on the way here. She's meeting her fiancé in town to marry."

Nancy smiled. "Was she the young lady you were talking to in the station?"

"She was," he said.

The woman continued while Jake climbed from the seat into her lap. "Did she mention who her new husband was? Chuck might know him."

Heaven knew Josie had said the man's name enough to tire anyone, yet, Quincy had no idea what his surname was. "Wilbert is what I remember. I can't seem to recall his last name."

The Morgans exchanged puzzled looks until Chuck said, "He must live a ways from Sacramento or merely keeps to himself."

"Had they met before today?" Nancy wanted to know.

"No, she was something of a mail order bride. They'd written several letters, but he'd never traveled to Baltimore, and this was her first trip west."

Distracted by an oncoming wagon, Chuck absently said, "If they've corresponded so much, I'm sure she's safe with him."

The fine hairs on the back of Quincy's neck rose much like the dust surrounding them from wheels on the hard road. "I'm sure," he managed to reply without feeling the words. Wilbert could be any sort of man from the best in California to the worst. Yet, Quincy had left Josie to her fate without vetting her new husband. "She seemed like a smart girl," he mumbled, hoping to convince himself he hadn't made a terrible mistake in leaving her behind.

"Mr. Easton?" Nancy began. "You seem rather uneasy."

Chuck nodded, turning in his seat before slowing the horses. "Are you fretting over your young lady?"

"Of course, he is." His wife reached over and repositioned a squirming Jake in her lap. "Let's show him the boys' new home so he can return to town."

He liked her idea, yet leaving the boys so soon felt irresponsible of him. "I do need to make sure the children are settled."

Chuck hopped off the wagon and opened the gate. "This is our home. Their home, too." He strolled over to Quincy. "Go on back to town, check up on your young lady, and come back tomorrow. We'll give you the grand tour and feed you a meal or two before sending you back east."

Quincy examined the boys' reactions to the mention of him leaving them here. Mike yawned while Jake napped in Nancy's arms. Satisfied the children liked where they were, he said, "Very well. Count on me returning for dinner at noon."

CHAPTER 6

JOSIE'S HAND TREMBLED AS SHE POURED THE LAST BIT of coffee into her cup. A lady never cursed, true, but she felt very close to throwing a tantrum. Her stomach rumbled. The gurgles echoed in the empty room. Where on earth was Wilbert? Had he mixed up the date and time? She took her coffee, finding a seat facing the entrance. No one had been in or out since the last passenger left the station.

She glanced over at the stationmaster only to find him glaring at her. Josie couldn't blame him. Both were being inconvenienced by Wilbert's awful tardiness. She tried to resist glancing at the large clock and failed. The five minutes since the last time she'd looked felt like an hour's length. Her behind ached from the hard seat. She sipped the last few drops of coffee, debating on whether to rinse the cup for the next person. What if Wilbert came in while she was busy and didn't see her?

After picking up her bag, she went to the refreshment station, wiping her cup clean with a dishcloth. Quincy wouldn't have left her waiting. He didn't seem to be the type of man to keep anyone inconvenienced for so long. She gave her head a slight shake to dislodge the disloyal thought. The two men couldn't compare. Wilbert was a farmer, used to following nature and the seasons. Quincy lived by train schedules and adoption paperwork. There was no need to fall further into the trap of thinking such disparaging thoughts about her future husband. She needed to focus on how she'd greet him once he walked into the depot for her.

A train's whistle sounded to the east. "That'll be the last for the day." The stationmaster opened the doors. "You're welcome to stay until the passengers are gone, but only until then. I'll need to lock up for the night."

Worry pierced her. When the depot closed, where would she go? She couldn't think about that now and tried to smile. "Thank you. I'm sure my fiancé will be here soon."

"Hmph," the guy grunted. "What did you say his name was again? Maybe misheard."

"Wilbert Peppers."

"Peppers? Nope. No one around here has that name. Wilbert, either. Are you sure someone isn't playing a game with you?"

Imagining some unknown man laughing at her falling for his ruse froze Josie's blood. It was bad enough for her to dwell on his irresponsible tardiness. She never considered his letters and love to be a cruel prank. "N-no," she stammered. "He's a fine young man who's very mistaken about my arrival is all."

"I'm sure you're right." He left to help with the train as people began streaming into the station from the platform. Josie watched as almost every passenger met their party. Those without someone to greet them strode through the lobby purposefully before leaving through the opposite side. She failed to stop fidgeting while watching the front door, hoping Wilbert had mistaken her train for the one currently at the station.

The minutes passed as Josie paced in front of the windows facing the main street. If Wilbert were truly pranking her, she found no humor in his actions at all. Even worse than the stationmaster asking her to leave was how low the sun hovered over the horizon. Long shadows from the western buildings stretched down the street. Even though spring had arrived, the warm temperatures hadn't received the telegraph to show up, too.

"Miss? It's time."

She faced the older man. "I understand. Would you be fine with me waiting outside?"

"Of course. Just stay safe and don't talk to strangers unless you're marrying them."

Josie didn't share his laugh. Instead, she followed him out of the station and watched as he locked up. His joke would be funny at any other time except now. "Thank you. I'll keep your advice in mind."

"You'll find hotels all up and down the street if you need one. I'll keep an eye out for this Peppers man tomorrow. Tell him you're here." The stationmaster tipped his hat. "Evening, and take care."

"You too." She watched for a moment as he headed down the boardwalk. A bench sat outside. She considered having a seat but decided against submitting her behind to further discomfort. A cool breeze stirred up dust and raised the brim of her bonnet a little as it swept by her. She shivered, having a couple of hours until darkness. If Wilbert didn't show up until tomorrow, she'd spend a cold night on the bench.

The traffic of buggies, wagons, and horses had slowed since she'd watched Quincy leave with the family. Her stomach growled. Josie looked up the street left first, then right. She hadn't planned on needing a hotel room at all, counting on her fiancé being here by now. Enough of her funds remained for one supper, at least.

She started for the nearest hotel. After a nice meal, the place might let her wait in the lobby until the station opened tomorrow. Then, she'd tell Wilbert what she thought of his tardiness. Standing outside of the hotel, she paused. Except, she couldn't. The man was her only shelter in the world. If she angered him with her own ire, he'd likely not marry her. Not that she needed a man, not even a kind one like Quincy. But with Aunt Erma all but forbidding her to return, Josie didn't have a choice. She'd need to find her wayward Wilbert or suitable employment as soon as possible.

"Miss Simmons?"

Josie whirled around at Quincy's voice. Happiness filled her at seeing his friendly face, and she almost hugged him in relief. "Mr. Easton?" She couldn't resist teasing him. "I thought we'd agreed to less formal names."

"So we did." He looked at their surroundings. "Do I have the chance to meet your husband?"

The shame of being yet unmarried fought with her delight in meeting him again. "No, I'm afraid not. He's mixed up the dates, I suspect, and I'll meet him tomorrow. Probably."

Quincy frowned. "You don't sound certain."

She swallowed, ashamed to confess, "I'm not."

CHAPTER 7

Quincy resisted the sudden need to take Josie in his arms to comfort her. He hadn't missed the slight tremble of her lower lip after her admission. "Mr. Peppers didn't leave a message at the station?"

"No, none."

Heaven help Wilbert for making his intended wait for so long alone. Quincy would wring the man's neck like he was a scrawny chicken. "Very well. I'm starving, and I know you must be, too. Let's go inside, have dinner, and discuss what you want to do next."

"I don't know..." she began.

He couldn't let her argue her way out of a meal. Plus, she desperately needed the protection, even if she wouldn't admit to such a thing. "I do, and I won't take anything but 'yes, Mr. Easton, I'd love to dine with you' as an answer."

Sensing a softening in Josie's expression, he pressed further. "I already have a long trip back to Chicago by myself. Will you keep me from dining alone tonight, at least?"

Josie's cheeks flushed as she gave him a smile. "You leave me no choice. It's my good deed for the day."

He held out his arm for her with a grin. "Excellent." Suddenly shy, he led her into the hotel. The restaurant smells hit him, making his stomach rumble. He figured Josie had to be far hungrier since he'd noticed how she'd eaten like a bird at every meal on the train. "I want one of everything they're serving."

"So do I." She let her arm fall from his, gripping her bag with both hands. The lobby appeared grand with polished wood and tile floors. Their footsteps echoed as they approached the restaurant doors. "Do you think they'll let me wash dishes if I order extra?"

Quincy wasn't sure if she meant her comment or was teasing. "Maybe, but I don't think it'll be necessary. I'll share it with you."

She waited as he held open the door for her. "I wouldn't ask you to, but I certainly wouldn't refuse."

Quincy caught the eye of a waitress. She nodded with a smile before pointing to an empty table. He followed her instructions and led Josie to their seats. Pulling out her chair, he said, "Do feel free to order anything you want. A gentleman always pays when asking a lady out for dinner."

Josie put her bag on the floor close to her feet. Folding her hands in her lap, she asked, "Even an engaged one?"

"Even an engaged one." Before he could acknowledge feelings about her impending marriage, the waitress came over to them.

"Welcome to the Barnaby. Our special today is roast beef with the trimmings. Dessert du jour is apple pie, chocolate cake, and peach turnovers."

Quincy raised his eyebrows at Josie. "The special is fine for me. Would you like a slice of apple pie to share?"

"Yes, and I'd like the special too, please," she replied.

He smiled at the server. "Could we have water also?"

"Of course." She finished scribbling down their order, leaving for the kitchen soon after.

As soon as the waitress was out of earshot, he addressed Josie. "I'll tell you about the boys' new home and how I'm going back tomorrow if you'll tell me about your day."

Josie leaned back in her chair just enough to make the wood squeak in protest. "There's not much to say." Not meeting his eyes, she continued. "I had nothing to do but wait and hope I didn't miss Wilbert if he came in to find me."

Another flash of irritation swept through Quincy. He tried to keep his tone even as he asked, "Did you ask the stationmaster if he knew who Wilbert was?"

Nodding, she took off her bonnet before laying a napkin

across her lap. "I did. Not only had he never heard of him, but he was also quite terse about my asking."

A small-town railroad employee being rude to Josie angered him. "Do I need to have a talk with him tomorrow about how to treat a lady?"

She stopped, waiting for a different server to pass by their table before adding, "He wasn't mean, just busy."

Their waitress approached with drinks, or he'd argue the point. Quincy waited until she'd given them their waters and left. Deciding to change the subject from Wilbert's ineptitude to his future intentions towards her, he asked, "What if your intended doesn't come for you tomorrow? Do you have friends to stay with until he decides to retrieve you?"

A few seconds passed. She stared at the salt and pepper shakers as if in a trance. "No, I don't know anyone but Wilbert." She glanced up as if someone had waved a hand between her and the centerpiece to break the spell. "And you, until you're on the train back east. I know you must think I've been foolish in coming out here without an alternate plan, and you'd be right. Going by the letters he sent, I had no idea he was anything but completely devoted to me." Her gaze dropped, shielding her eyes from his view. "The trip out here took everything I had and then some."

A protective instinct rushed through him so hard, his hand trembled. He reached for his glass to steady his emotions. Josie had traveled across the country on a penny and a promise, and now? If Wilbert didn't step up before Quincy left, Josie would have to make her way in a strange city. All sorts of horrible things ran through his mind. Terrible events from his time on the streets as a young boy. "No," he said aloud, stopped by their waitress coming up with their food.

She set one plate in front of Josie and the other in front of him. "There you are. Two specials."

"Thank you," Josie replied, not wasting any time before taking her first bite.

Another customer caught the server's attention, and she left to care for them. Quincy gave her the briefest of notice as he watched Josie dig into her roast beef. As soon as he took a bite, he understood her bliss. The meat was perfectly tender with the gravy salted just right. New potatoes and carrots completed the meal. Hungrier than he'd figured, he appreciated the quiet between them as they ate. Josie had good table manners. His Sisters at the orphanage would have been proud of her. Yet, he noticed she didn't pause much between bites. She also never let go of her fork. Despite his efforts to share with her on the train, he figured she'd been half-starved the entire way.

Quincy swallowed and took a drink of water before asking, "Did he give you any money at all? Did he even offer?"

"Hm um," she hummed before doing the same as Quincy and taking a sip. "No, and I didn't ask. He'd had a horrible year last year with the crops. I didn't want to be a financial burden before we had even married." She wiped her mouth with a napkin. "The trip was difficult on minimal funds, but not as much as traveling here by stagecoach or even wagon train."

He knew he was prying too much into her affairs but couldn't keep from asking, "Have you thought about your plans if Wilbert never retrieves you?"

Josie's fork stopped midway between her plate and her mouth and hovered for a moment. "No," she finally replied. "If I'm not at his farm by this time tomorrow, I'll devise a plan of finding work and a place to live." She finished her bite.

Watching her eat, his stomach soured at the thought of her here in Sacramento. She'd be alone and depending on strangers. Not that he wasn't more than barely a friend, of course. He took a drink. At least he was a man who'd be kind to her and not some sly dog off the street. Their waitress caught his eye as she approached with a dessert. Before she could get too far, he held up two fingers. She smiled, nodded, and went back to the kitchen.

Quincy figured he had two things to accomplish tomorrow. Hours in a day dictated either one task or another could happen, but not both. First, he needed to visit Jake and Mike in their new home one more time. Or second, he needed to wait with Josie until Wilbert decided to make an appearance. At this point, he reckoned the man had to be either dead or a chicken. Otherwise, he would never have abandoned his fiancée like this.

Josie was mopping her plate with the last bit of her dinner roll when the server set down their desserts. Looking from the waitress to Quincy, she frowned. "Two? You signaled for both pies?"

"I did." He grinned at their server. "Thank you."

The woman returned his smile. "I'll refill your glasses, too."

Before he could reply, she'd turned on her heel and left. He ate the last carrot, hoping Sister Margaret was proud in absentia and pushed the plate aside in favor of apple pie. "I know you wanted to share, but I don't. You've skimped enough in the past few days and can handle my treating you."

She picked at the flaky crust. "This isn't a treat. This is you, trying to adopt me to raise as one of your orphans."

Quincy waited until their glasses were filled and the server closer to the kitchen. "You are anything but a child to me, Josie. All I want to do is hunt down and punch your absent fiancé before sending you back to Baltimore."

"I'm not going back home, ever, but would like front

row seats to the fight." She took another bite, giving a little hum at the taste.

"Hunger makes the best sauce." He dug into the crust's edge. "I'm sad to be almost done."

"So am I." She set down her fork, folding her hands in her lap. "If I'd been thinking, I'd have wrapped my dinner roll in my napkin."

"Like you did on the train?"

Josie gave him a wry smile. "Not quite. I brought the food with me, bread, cheese, apples. Uncle George's flask worked for water. I didn't know the newer trains provided any."

Their waitress came up with the ticket. "You can pay when you're ready. We're slow tonight, so there's no hurry."

"Thank you." Quincy waited until she walked away before pulling the money from his pocket. "And, thank you for letting me take care of dinner."

Her cheeks flushed as she looked away from him. "You're welcome, and I'm very grateful."

Josie's anxious expression as she examined their surroundings tugged at his heart. He placed the money on the ticket with a little extra for the service. His bet was she worried about where to stay tonight. The restaurant would be closing soon. The hotel seemed too fancy to let anyone, even ladies like her, remain in the lobby overnight. He had an idea, improper, but practical. "Let's see if I can get a room here. Would you like to see what sort of accommodations a place like this has?"

She chuckled. "I don't think I should, though your attempt to lure me in is a good one."

"Oh, come on." Quincy stood, an idea taking root in his mind. "Let's see what they offer here. You can come up, see how well-to-do people live, and then continue on with whatever you'd planned for the rest of the night." She bit her lip at his last words while retrieving her bonnet and carpetbag. Striking a nerve in her about the dire situation hurt him, too, but was necessary for her own good. He grabbed his overnight bag and headed for the lobby, sure she'd follow.

He strolled up to the registration counter, and the clerk waiting there. "Good evening. I would like a room for tonight, if possible."

"It is." The young man licked a finger, turning a page in the guest registry. "One of our smaller rooms is available." He glanced up at the two of them. "The bed is big enough for you and your wife, but only just."

"No, we're not married," Josie said before Quincy could stop her. "My friend here merely wanted to show me what a fine hotel like this offered its guests."

"Ah, well." The clerk closed the book. "We don't let rooms to unmarried couples under any circumstances. Illicit activities aren't allowed on-premise, hotel policy."

Trying to salvage the situation and provide Josie a safe place to sleep tonight, Quincy forced a laugh. "You caught us fair and square." He took her hand. "We're not married, yet, because she arrived after the justice of the peace closed for the day. We're saying our vows tomorrow and celebrating our wedding night then."

"Good and congratulations. Do you have proof of your intentions?" he asked. Quincy couldn't lie, shaking his head. With a little smirk, the clerk continued, "I thought so. Good attempt, but only one of you can have the last room tonight."

CHAPTER 8

Josie could accept leaving Quincy behind in his hotel room. She'd become accustomed to the thought of sleeping on the bench outside of the depot tonight. Except, the stricken look on Quincy's face when he glanced at her changed her mind to simply leave him at the hotel. A solution lay at the bottom of her carpetbag and would get them this room, she was sure of it. She opened up the bag and began digging. "Here, I have proof we were supposed to be married today." Feeling the letter, she pulled it from under her work dress. "It's my proposal from Wil," she glanced at Quincy. "Right, Wil?"

The clerk took the paper from her, giving it a quick read. Before Quincy could protest, the clerk smiled, "So you're Wil Peppers?"

"He is. Haven't you met?" Josie replied. "Honey," she addressed Quincy. "I thought you were more of a man about town than this."

"I don't know everyone," Quincy stammered.

By now, the clerk had the guest book open again. "Since you have a letter of intent, I can let the rules slide this once." He spun the book around to face them, giving him the pen. "I fully expect you to spend tomorrow night here, too."

"We will unless our families insist we stay with them," Josie said, looping her arm in Quincy's free one as he wrote their names as Mr. and Mrs. Wil Peppers. "Who can control what a mother-in-law wants?"

Giving her a nod, the clerk slid a key over to Quincy. "I wouldn't even try. You'll be in room 207 at the end."

Quincy took the key without a word, gesturing for Josie to go ahead. She did so, heading for the stairs. Once up half a flight in the stairwell, she felt comfortable enough to whisper, "I didn't think my plan would work so well with him."

"I'll admit I was surprised. Not that I hadn't thought about marrying you, but I never considered being Wilbert."

She stumbled over the last step, using the rail to catch herself. Quincy had said, what, exactly? "I'm sorry, marry me?"

Quincy walked past her and into the hallway. "If doing so gave you a safe and warm place to sleep tonight, then yes. I'd marry you."

Stunned, she followed him down the call and sputtered, "But, you couldn't. We hardly know each other."

He turned the key in the lock. "And you had a perfect piece of evidence, so I didn't need to propose." He swung the door open. "Let's see what Wilbert's letter procured for us, shall we?"

Quincy let her step in first. An oil lamp with a low flame pushed against the dark. Josie noted how her room at Aunt Erma's was larger. But the hotel's bedrooms were far less of a prison. The bed took up most of the room with a chair and end table, further reducing the floor space. She liked it well enough and hoped the charge wasn't too much. Pressing on the bed, she ran her fingertips over the soft covers. "Very nice. You'll be comfortable here."

"We will." He set his bag down on the wooden chair. "I plan on sharing with you."

Faking an engagement was one thing, spending a night with a handsome adoption agent quite another. Their one kiss in the closet had proved how flimsy her self-control around him was. "Plan again, Mr. Easton." She grabbed her bag, heading for the exit. "I've seen and appreciated the luxury but do need to leave."

Quincy went to the door, blocking her way. "No, you don't. I refuse to let you stay outside tonight where anyone could harm you." Before she could protest, he took her arm, his hand gentle. "Tell me you'd feel safer out there than in here with me. Say the words that you don't believe my promise to simply let you sleep."

He was right. She couldn't. Except, spending the night here with him would be far too tempting. Goosebumps rose on her arms at the intimate possibilities between them. She managed to squeak, "But where would you be? In bed with me?"

"As much as I'd like to be, no." He pulled a blanket from the foot of the bed before grabbing one of the pillows. "I've spent nights in far worse places than on a wood floor in a nice hotel." He winked at her before laying out the blanket in a pallet. "Spent time with far worse people, too."

She watched, horrified, as he began making himself comfortable next to the bed. "I can't just let you sleep on the floor." She pulled off the top covers. "And I can't just let you sleep there, either. Take this, too. You'll want the extra cushion under you."

He shook his head, ignoring her offer. "You'll be left with just a sheet to keep you warm."

"You're sleeping on the cold ground, so I think I have the better end of the deal." She squinted at the blankets he was trying to smooth. "In fact, I almost have a better idea. If you can keep to yourself, we could roll a blanket between us and use it as a divider. That way, we'd both get the bed."

He got onto his knees, tilting his head. "I don't know. Can you keep your hands to yourself?"

"Excuse me?" she gasped.

"I'm a man in my prime, and you?" He shrugged, getting to his feet. "You're just a woman."

The teasing tone in his voice didn't fool her. Still, she couldn't help but chuckle. "Somehow, I'll muddle through."

"All right, then." He began rolling up one blanket and placed it in a line bisecting the bed. "We'll see how long you can resist me before I give up and go back to the floor."

Josie laughed, even if what he'd said was a tiny bit true. He was rather attractive. Even more so now she knew how his lips felt against hers. She shivered, setting her bag down on her side of the bed, removing her bonnet and unlacing her boots. He spread the other blanket over the bed. She peeled off her socks, wiggling her toes. Despite the playful banter between them, she didn't feel comfortable changing into a nightgown.

"I can turn around if you need some privacy," he offered as if reading her mind. Undoing the top two buttons of his collar, he also unbuttoned his cuffs. Josie looked away in case he decided to remove his shirt entirely. He said, "I don't want to make you feel uncomfortable."

Wearing a nightgown would be a welcome change from

her dress, still dirty from her train ride. She glanced around the room and, seeing no mirrors, replied, "I'd appreciate your doing so whenever you're ready."

He faced away from her. She waited for a second before turning her back to him, too. With her gown in hand, she removed her dress and undergarment, wishing she had facilities for a bath. Maybe later, when or if Wilbert ever took her home. As soon as the nightgown settled down to her ankles, she turned to him again. "There. I'm done." She slid under the covers. "You could turn down the lamp before getting into bed."

"Good idea." He twisted the small wheel, lowering the wick. Settling onto his side and facing Josie, he gave her a smile. "Are you still good with sharing a bed?"

"As long as the blanket roll stays in place, it's fine." Quincy punched the pillow into a comfortable place for his head. Josie wanted to know more about his day, and when he was settled, she asked, "You mentioned visiting Jake and Mike tomorrow?" she asked, and he nodded. "Did you see their home at all?"

"I did. The Morgans live on a large farm with the main house and several smaller buildings. The entire setup looks prosperous. I'm almost jealous of the two."

"Wonder if the Morgans will consider adopting an older boy like you."

Quincy chuckled. "I'd thought about asking, but then what would the Sisters of Mercy do without me? They have the other agent, Bran, but need all the help they can get." He tucked a hand under his face. "Speaking of help, what will you do if Wilbert doesn't come for you by this time tomorrow? Do you want my assistance in planning your next steps? I could lend you train fare back home."

He'd voiced her worst fear. Josie closed her eyes, resisting the urge to hide her face in the pillow. "You're right, I need some sort of plan for life on my own."

He put a hand on her arm before withdrawing. "Without being too forward, my offer of marriage still stands."

His offer soothed her. Quincy had a kind soul for giving her a solution so binding. Still, she couldn't let him throw his life away on her. Wilbert was also a good reason to refuse, she remembered a little too late. She opened her eyes and smiled to soften her response. "I appreciate your gesture, but no. By this time tomorrow, I'll be Wilbert's wife, not yours."

"I hope you're right." He pulled the blanket over his shoulder. "Just...know that you're welcome to come back to Chicago with me as my wife if necessary. We'd remain friends at first if the idea of being with me troubles you."

Josie couldn't meet his stare. "I must confess. Between

your compassion to me and care for Jake and Mike, I struggle to remember who my fiancé is. You've been a gentleman, a friend, and if I were honest, I'd marry you first thing tomorrow morning."

"I hear an 'except' in your admission."

"I owe Wilbert a chance to explain his tardiness," she said, and the hopeful expression faded from his face. "I made a promise to him, and despite my infatuation for you, I still feel very deeply for him." When the words left her, hovering between her and Quincy, she realized they weren't true anymore. Loving someone on paper proved far too difficult when an even better man cared for her in person.

His smile taut, Quincy said, "You're taking my proposal far more seriously than I'd intended. My offer was merely to provide protection and a home. I think you're a fine woman, but clearly, we're just friends." He turned over, facing away from her. "So, good night. See you in the morning."

She took a marriage proposal too seriously? Was he mad? How else was a woman supposed to take it? She turned over as well, frowning at the dimly lit wall. Weariness hit her all of a sudden. The handsome man sleeping next to her clearly had a hero streak a mile wide. She needed to wake up enough to tell him not everyone needed a hero.

Josie opened her eyes, disoriented at first. The room looked nothing like the one she'd left in Baltimore. Midmorning sunlight streamed in through the window's lace curtains. Where was Quincy, she wondered in a bit of a panic. His side of the bed was flat, yet she could only suspect he'd gone while she slept. Rolling over to his side, she searched for and saw his travel bag still on the floor. Wherever he was, she figured he had to come back sometime.

She lay there for a few moments more, fighting the urge to fall back asleep. They'd gone to bed without cleaning up at all. Or, at least she had. A long hot bath would have to wait until Wilbert took her home. She'd never thought to ask him if he had a washtub big enough. All their letters had been about feelings instead of practical things. She left the bed, finding and opening her travel bag. With a dirty napkin in hand, she headed for the pitcher of water and washbasin on the small table.

Blinking a few times at the bread roll, a hunk of cheese, and tiny jelly jar on a plate, she smiled at Quincy's thoughtfulness. Even better, he'd provided a butter knife and a pat of butter for the roll. She put a hand over the cup of coffee to find it still hot. A private breakfast for her wasn't a grand gesture, no, but her heart sang anyway.

However they had gone to sleep last night, he still cared for her.

Soon, Josie had her face and other parts refreshed from a newly washed napkin. She had also nibbled at the food until the plate was clean, too. Changing into her work dress took no time at all. Their room lacked a mirror, so she had to style her hair the best she could from memory. Too bad for Wilbert if he'd wanted to see her better attired. He should have been here yesterday. A knock at the door interrupted her putting on socks. "Yes?"

"Are you decent?" Quincy asked through the solid wood.

"I am." She finished pulling on her second shoe as he entered the room. "I didn't mean to sleep so long. Are we due to check out soon?"

He came over to sit beside her, a newspaper tucked under his arm. "In a couple of hours, and I don't mind. You needed the rest."

"Thank you for letting me." She searched his face. He didn't seem his usual almost too chipper self like he'd been prior mornings on the train. "Is everything all right?

"Yes, for the most part. The agency expects me in Chicago soon. There's another group of children and homes who want them."

"How is that not wonderful?"

"It's perfect for me, and yet?" He stood and went to

look out of the window. "I couldn't move anywhere else but there if I wanted to help the Sisters of Mercy place children."

"Why can't you be an adoption agent for anyone else?" Josie asked.

"Oh, I could and would be happy." Quincy paused for a moment, pulling back the lace curtain. "My only problem is I want to stay here with you, and it's not possible. Even if you didn't marry Wilbert, there's not enough demand for children here."

"I find that hard to believe in a city like Sacramento." She went to him. "It's large with enough farmland around. Maybe if you put an ad in the newspaper?"

"I've been scanning the paper already. Several other agencies have representatives here culled from the locals." He stopped staring out of the window to look at her. "I can't kiss another man's woman in a hotel room, yet, it's all I want to do. When I woke up to find you beside me? We'd merely spent an innocent night together, nothing extraordinary. After seeing you smile in your sleep, though, I want to greet every morning with you."

Quincy moved around her to the foot of the bed before grabbing his overnight bag. "That's why we need to find Wilbert soon. I need to get back home now, so meet me in the lobby when you're ready to go."

He both left the room and left her puzzled. Did this

mean he'd been serious about marrying her? Impossible, since they'd met a handful of days ago. And yet, every morning with him might be like today? She shoved her nightgown and damp napkin into her bag, grabbing her bonnet and hurrying after him.

CHAPTER 9

Quincy didn't have much time to pace the lobby before spying Josie as she rushed down the stairs. She spotted him at the other end of the large room and smiled. The relieved expression on her face gave his heart a twinge. How could she suspect he'd leave her here? Certainly, he might have hurried out on errands this morning for the orphanage's sake but still. He'd explicitly said he'd be waiting for her here. As she approached, he said, "I've reserved us a room for tonight, if necessary. I'll need one at least, and you're welcome again in case your fiancé hasn't taken you home with him."

"He will," she asserted before adding, "He simply must."

Unwilling to argue, Quincy opened the main door

instead, asking, "Would you want to visit Jake and Mike with me?"

For a second, she bit a lip he found infinitely kissable and said, "Yes, but no. As much as I'd love to see the boys again, letting Wilbert find me is too important." She took his arm as they headed down the boardwalk to the livery stable. "You don't intend to stay here forever, so I either need to marry him or find decent work."

He examined Josie's face, her cheeks flushed in the cold morning air. Her steps sounded on the boards like a march. He wanted nothing more than to pull her back to the hotel, out of sight from the general rabble, and beg her to forget about Wilbert. As soon as a group of oncoming ladies passed out of earshot, he asked, "Do you still want to marry the man? Think before you answer. If I were him, I'd have been camped out on the station's platform and waiting for the instant your train left Baltimore."

"Well, you're obviously a very romantic and impractical man who isn't running a farm." She stopped with him in front of the livery. "I'll be at the depot until it closes unless Wilbert finds me first."

He needed to break through her denial of being left by Wilbert. Once again, he offered, "If he doesn't, would you want to stay at the hotel again under the same conditions as before?"

Her cheeks reddened before she looked away, unable to meet his gaze. "Yes, please. I'd be grateful and would find a way to pay my share when I can."

"We can argue about money later over dinner," he teased. "I've heard most couples do their best fighting about funds over a nice meal."

Josie laughed. "Very well, I almost look forward to our argument. Take care."

He held out his hand, and she took it, giving a little gasp when he kissed the back of her fingers. "So do I." Letting go of her, he took a card from his pocket. The small rectangle might be a little bent, but his address at the Sisters of Mercy was still evident. "If we don't meet again today and you *ever* need anything, contact me here."

She took his card, reading his address at the agency. "What if you're out delivering orphans to their new homes? I don't want to bother you."

"They'll either find me, or I'll return and read your message for myself." He put his hands in his pockets to resist hugging her. "I know you don't have your new address yet. Feel free to write a letter and let me know if married life is all you dreamed it would be."

"I think this is the nicest thing anyone's ever done for me." Her eyes filled with tears, and she cleared her throat. "I mean, yesterday at dinner and afterward was so very kind, too, but now? I very much appreciate your concern." She put the card in a book resting in her bag. "You'll get a letter the instant I'm settled in my new home."

"Good." A train's whistle broke through the various other noises. "I'd better hire a horse for the ride out."

She nodded, a sad smile on her lips. "And I should wait."

His throat seemed closed as he croaked, "Goodbye, Josie. It's been a pleasure to know you."

"Likewise, Quincy." She stood a little straighter before leaving for the station.

The steam from the locomotive approached. Quincy wanted to run after her but kept his feet planted until seeing her walk into the depot. As if broken from a trance, he shook his head and went into the livery stable. The prices for horses, buggies, and wagons were scrawled in chalk on a blackboard. He tried to focus on the task at hand. Economically, a horse would be best. Unless the adoption wasn't working out for either the new parents or the children. Then only a buggy would do. He wouldn't trust any old horse to carry him, Jake, and Mike sitting on one saddle.

After a wait, a buggy was brought around to the front for Quincy. "Thank you," he said to the stable boy before giving him a tip. He seated himself, giving one last glance at the train station. They'd said their goodbyes a little more than a quarter-hour ago. All he wanted was to scoop her up and drop her onto his buggy seat. Then ride with her in any direction except Wilbert's.

Quincy couldn't make himself snap the reins to leave her, but the boys depended on him. The orphans back in Chicago also needed him to find new homes for them. The Sisters trusted him to carry out their orphanage's mission. The one person in the world he wanted to rely on him, Josie, instead wanted another man to be her everything.

People and carriages flowed around him as he thought, or did she genuinely want Wilbert? After all, she *had* spent the night in bed with Quincy. Innocently sleeping, yes, but in a bed nonetheless. He'd watched her face in the early dawn before duty called him to the telegraph office. She'd been so lovely, smiling during a dream. Her skin tempted a slight caress from him before he quickly dressed and left the room. He'd had his breakfast, bringing back hers. She'd still slept, exhausted, he knew, from the scant rest she'd had on the train ride here.

Wilbert didn't deserve her. The man had let his future wife travel across the continent on insufficient funds in case of an emergency. Quincy frowned at all the disasters filling his imagination. No woman of his would ever do without in such a stark way. She'd have the best sleeper cars and hotel rooms he could provide her.

The train whistle as it left the station cut through the

noise around Quincy, pushing him into action. Josie needed to realize Wilbert might never show up for her. Even more important than anything else, *he* needed her as much as she needed him. Snapping the reins, he drove the buggy over to the train station. A small family exited the building as he pulled up. Quickly tying off the horse, he hurried in, praying she still waited inside. He'd only spent a little while away from her. If she'd left with her fiancé already, Quincy figured he would have noticed her even from a city block away.

Only, the empty depot echoed his footsteps. One younger man sat behind a counter. Quincy went to the restroom door and listened for a minute. No noises indicating Josie might be in there. Now the station clerk was looking at him from where he sat. Quincy nodded in greeting before going to the train platform, hoping she was sitting on a bench outside. It was a long shot because Wilbert would be walking in the front door, not the back. Sure enough, she wasn't there either.

Quincy had one last thing to do before losing all hope. Strolling up to the counter, he asked, "I wonder if you can help me."

"I can try. Who are you looking for?"

"A woman," he blurted out before thinking about the request.

The clerk sighed, propping his chin up with his elbow on the counter. "So, aren't we all."

"Pardon, but I'm looking for a particular lady who was in here not even a half-hour ago. She's as tall as here." He raised his hand up to nose level. "She's wearing a green dress matching her eyes, has blonde hair…" He paused just short of admitting Josie was the most beautiful woman in the world.

"I did see her. She came up and asked about someone. I didn't know who he was, and she waited for a little while." He leaned back in his chair. "Then, the train arrived. I was busy, too busy to see her leave. I assumed she met whoever she knew and left with him."

Quincy had the same feeling as to why she wasn't here. The realization over how she'd met Wilbert had seemed unreal until this very minute. His heart felt torn apart in his chest. "Thank you. Have a good day."

"You too, mister. Sorry I couldn't be of more help."

He nodded, absently going for the door. In the distant part of his practical side, he needed to visit the boys before going back home. The Sisters expected him to ensure the Morgans were the best parents possible. Yet, his body didn't seem to obey his mind's directive to get on the buggy and go already. From on the high seat, he searched the area for her to no avail. She was gone. He'd missed his last chance to beg she forget about Wilbert and come home with him.

Quincy shook his head. Mike and Jake. He needed to stay focused on his duty, instead of allowing his haze of pain to distract him. What his heart wanted didn't matter anymore. Like the dreaded death of a loved one you don't believe can genuinely happen, Josie was gone.

CHAPTER 10

Josie paced the train station. She'd asked the stationmaster earlier about Wilbert Peppers to no avail. Her travel bag seemed heavy, so she set it down on the nearby bench. Facing the windows, she'd be able to see if Wilbert approached. The last few passengers meandered out with their families, leaving her alone, or almost. A young man not much older than her sat behind a desk, his nose in a book. He hadn't looked up since she'd arrived here. She wanted to ask him if he'd seen anyone matching Wilbert's description. As inattentive as he was, she figured he wouldn't have a good answer.

Frustrated, she picked up her bag before going out of the front door. She couldn't loiter in the station all day, waiting for a man who may or may not show up. The post office was a few doors down. She'd write him a letter, post it, and hope

Quincy might let her ride with him to the boys' new home. A couple of fresh sheets of paper were folded in her book. She'd need to borrow a pen from the postmaster. The one envelope she'd used to hold all of Wilbert's letters had his return address. A stamp might cost her the last few pennies she had, but if he finally came for her, the expense would be worth it.

She walked into the post office, grateful for the warmth. Mornings here were a lot cooler than at home. A potbellied stove sat in the center. Several people milled about, getting mail or being helped by the postmaster. She sighed in relief at spotting a small table with an inkwell sitting in the corner next to a window. Going to the writing area, she retrieved a piece of paper from the book before setting down her bag.

What to say to an absent fiancé? One who should have met her train the instant the first wheels rolled into the station? She took one of the pens and dipped it in ink. A drop fell back into the inkwell. The noise and chatter tumbled away as she planned out what to write to Wilbert. Despite her irritation, she wanted to avoid an angry tone. He might have had extenuating circumstances for not meeting her yesterday.

Josie's hand wavered, and she rested her wrist on the edge of the table. Yesterday? She'd spent the night with Quincy, and yet their time together already seemed so long ago. He was gone, now, delivering Jake and Mike to their new family. She redipped the pen. She and Wilbert would have a new family someday, too. Just as soon as he read the letter and knew she was in town already. Ignoring the longing in her heart for Quincy, she scribbled a brief note for Wilbert.

Dearest,

She paused, certain *Was I unclear about the date of my arrival?* seemed far too angry.

I've made a horrible mistake and told you the wrong date of my arrival, it seems. I'm here in Sacramento and eager to meet you at last.

Josie dipped the pen and reread her words. Yes, she was eager, eager to have a bed some near-stranger like Quincy didn't need to buy for her. Pushing aside her frustration, she continued.

Please come find me at the train station. I'll be here waiting for you to retrieve me at your earliest convenience.

Love,

Josie

She blotted the pen before placing it in the holder. Trying to keep her thoughts kind about when Wilbert's convenience might be, she watched the ink dry, blowing on the larger scribbles a few times to hurry the process. She'd written "love" without thinking. Signing her name with the affectionate term had been a habit by now. Yet, with so much hurt and ire in her heart, love didn't have room anymore.

Quincy's smile and tender ways with the boys flashed in her mind. No, love did have a place in her heart, but not for Wilbert.

"Ma'am, are you finished?"

An older gentleman in a top hat shook her from the daydream. "Oh, yes. Almost, sorry." She folded the letter into an envelope, hastily scribbling Wilbert's address from memory. She moved away from the table, grabbing her carpetbag along the way. Quincy was long gone and best forgotten. She'd mail the letter, go to the station, and wait for the man she'd meant to marry all along.

Once at the counter, she slid the letter to the postmaster and began digging for coins. "Hello, I'd like to send a letter, please."

"Sure, let me see where to." He stared at the address for a moment, frowning. "W. Peppers, huh?"

Josie nodded, finding a penny. Placing the money on the counter, she replied, "Yes, it's to my fiancé Wilbert."

The man's eyebrows rose to the middle of his forehead. "Wilbert? Is that his real name? No middle one, like 'son' or 'Bertson'?"

His odd reaction puzzled her. None of the clerks in Baltimore had ever quizzed her so much on letters sent to Wilbert before now. Maybe people out west had been out in the sun too long. Slowly, she said, "No, he didn't mention any middle name."

"Will, come out here," the man hollered, startling Josie.

"I'm sorting mail," came a muffled reply.

"It'll only take a minute," the postmaster yelled again. He smiled at Josie. "Sorry, he's a contrary old cuss. Even his wife says so." She returned his grin and waited for a few moments. The man's expression grew darker as he helped a couple of other people before returning to her. "Where the hell is that man? Will Bertson, a woman is waiting on you." Addressing Josie, he added, "The man loves the ladies."

A ringing in her ears kept her from replying. Will Bertson? Surely, Will Bertson couldn't be Wilbert, could he? If he were tall, lanky, with sandy blond hair and a hooked nose, he might be. Her heart pounded as the postmaster helped one last customer. She coughed to clear her throat. "I could come back later."

"Nonsense. I'll drag him up here for you because I think he's your man," he said. Before she could protest someone married couldn't be hers, he went to the door. "Will? Stop talking to that little ole gal out there and talk to this one in here." Coming back to her, he chuckled. "There's a young woman from Eldorado Hills who drops off her father's post office mail here for us. Will thinks he can charm anyone."

A shuffle at the door caught her attention, and sure

enough. Will Bertson and Wilbert Peppers were the same person. He gaped at her open-mouthed as she did the same at him. The postmaster interrupted their staring contest. "Have you two met?"

"In letters," Josie growled. "Why didn't you retrieve me from the train station, Wilbert?"

The cretin shrugged. "We were playing, Posie. You weren't supposed to actually come out here."

Playing what, she wondered until it hit her what he meant. All the wasted time and money on Wilbert, who couldn't even get her name correct? She clenched her teeth, grinding out, "It's Josie, you horrible man."

"All right," he muttered, edging toward the back room. "Anyway, I'd better get back to work."

Blocking the sorting room door, the postmaster grinned. "No, you can have a few minutes for a break. I want to see how you handle a little she-cat who's caught you at your game."

A small crowd had gathered around to witness the fuss. Josie tried to care, but her white-hot anger wouldn't let her. "If you were any sort of a decent man, I'd demand you marry me and take me home this instant."

The postmaster snorted a laugh. "Ethel might have something to say about that."

"Ethel?" she asked, already dreading the answer.

"Will's wife."

"You horrible, horrible man." She wadded up her letter and threw it at Will. "How many women have you lured out here to marry?" She mashed up the envelope stuffed full of his love letters to her. "You're a rotten, evil shyster who should be hanged."

Will's stance straightened as he went on the offensive. "It's your fault for coming out here. Nobody invited you."

Had he never sincerely asked her to be here? "You'd mentioned getting married in the spring. It's spring. What did you think I would do after I sent a letter about when I'd be here? Not show up?"

"Well, I had hoped you wouldn't."

"I'll bet," the postmaster snorted. "Ethel can be mean when other women come sniffing around him."

Will had a smug grin, wiping out any sort of attractiveness he ever might have had. She'd let Quincy go off into the future without her for this mutt of a man? "I see. Well, this is one woman who will never sniff around this pile of cow dung." She took her penny back, dropping the coin into her bag. "Thank you for your help, sir," she said to the postmaster. Turning on a heel, she left the post office in a fury.

Once outside in the bright morning, Josie strode to the train station as if she had a solid reason to go there. She pushed open the door with her chin held high, only stopping when at a long bench. Sitting, tears streamed down her eyes. She'd been more than stupid in coming out here on little to no funds. Every other mail-order bride could count on their future husband to come for them, but no, not her. She buried her face in her hands until the sobs built up enough to begin.

She felt a hand on her back before hearing Quincy's voice. "Josie?"

CHAPTER 11

If Quincy didn't turn around and head for the Morgans' farm this instant, he'd not be back in Sacramento until dusk. The Morgans would insist he stay with them for the night. His room might be paid for but would go unused, a waste of the orphan agency's money.

A woman in green rushing past caught his eye, and he stared. "Josie?" he whispered as she approached. Before he could wave, she disappeared into the depot. So, Wilbert hadn't picked her up after all. He hopped down from the buggy, intent on finding out why she looked ready to cry.

Inside the station, he found her seated in what had to be her favorite bench by now. She was sobbing in huge gulps, breaking his heart. He put a hand on her back. "Josie?"

She leaned against him, her face buried against his arm. Muffled, she said, "I met him. He was awful."

"What? How?"

"At the post office. He works there and is a horrible man." She leaned back, wiping her face. Quincy pulled a clean handkerchief from his pocket and gave it to her. "Thank you. He was a postal clerk, married to someone named Ethel. He was rude but correct. He'd asked me to marry him but never said to come here in person." She crumpled up the napkin in her hand, tears filling her eyes again. "I've made a horrible mistake both by coming here to marry him and not going to Chicago with you when I had the chance."

He opened his mouth to say she'd not made a mistake at all, but couldn't. Josie said she knew Wilbert better than she did Quincy, but was that the truth? She'd spent more alone time with him than with any other man, he'd bet. He stood, taking her hand to pull her up, too. "Wilbert might be a dead horse you couldn't race, but I'm still here for you, and so is Chicago if you'll have us."

She shook her head while scooping up her bag. "He wasn't even Wilbert. He's Will Bertson, and seems to have a habit of fooling women across the country."

He picked up her bag and began leading her toward the door. "Sounds criminal to me."

"It should be," she sobbed, stepping outside with him.

"I'm the only one who followed through on his proposal, he said. I feel so foolish for believing in him."

"You believed in love, and there's nothing wrong with doing so." Quincy put her bag next to his in the buggy.

Josie watched as he untied the horse from the hitch. "I'm not so sure, and you left your belongings out here where anyone could take them?" She took his hand, letting him help her up into the seat.

"If someone needs my bible and dirty clothes bad enough to steal them in broad daylight, they can have them." He found his place beside her. "I assume you're fine with visiting the boys. We can talk on the way there."

She leaned against him and sighed. "You assumed right. I've missed them. And you," she added as if an afterthought.

"But mostly them?" he teased, nudging her shoulder.

"Mostly both of you," Josie replied. She blinked a few times before moving a couple of inches away from him.

He glanced at her from the corner of his eyes. She now sat primly with her hands folded in her lap. Part of him wanted to know everything that happened when she finally met Wilb—just Will. The more considerate part of Quincy figured she'd tell him when the heartache had died down a little. "You know we're going to a farm. It's a little way outside of town. Do you have a brimmed hat to wear and keep the sun from burning your skin?"

"I do." She twisted around and brought her bag to the front. Opening it, she pulled out a bundle of cloth. "I made a sunbonnet from a pattern in a lady's magazine." She put on the hat, tying the strings. The wings on the bonnet hid her face completely. "My only problem is not being able to see anything."

"Here, I can fix this for you." Quincy put the reins between his knees to hold. He folded the wide brim back enough to clear her vision yet keep her shaded. She looked up into his eyes, and his heart beat faster. The world around them stopped as he said, "I'm sorry for what happened, but I'm glad you're not with another man after all."

Josie nodded slightly. "So am I. A clever woman would have forgotten her fiancé when you brought her breakfast on the train and, well—" Her face reddened. "Everywhere else besides."

So much of what she'd said in one sentence needed a discussion. They didn't have time today. Postponing an argument over her intelligence would have to wait. He planned to spend the rest of his life with her. "I tend to agree, but then I would." He picked up the reins and clicked at the horse. "What do women do when their hearts are broken?"

She shrugged before answering, "I suppose they visit newly adopted children."

Quincy laughed, enjoying her retort. "And have dinner with a fine young man like me?"

Josie gave him a sly glance. "If she's smart, she will."

"Good, then we have plans for this evening. We can dine, and I can tell you all how I'm a better fiancé than Wilbert ever could have been," he said, wondering how she'd respond to his bragging.

She held up a hand. "Oh, you don't need to say a word. I'm already convinced."

Quincy couldn't help but lean over and press his lips against her temple. "I'm glad," he said against the sun-heated bonnet.

Despite the warming day, a sudden cold breeze pushed against them. Josie shivered. "The land certainly is flat out here. Much more so than I expected."

"The Morgans live in the hills up ahead. At least, that's where their main homestead is. They've got a nice setup."

"Did they give you a tour?" she asked.

"Somewhat. I'd planned on being there the entire day today."

Josie was quiet for a few moments. Finally, she said, "You're kind in not adding until I delayed you."

"You didn't keep me in town." He took her hand and squeezed before letting go. "My need to see you one last time did."

"Even if I was with Wilbert?"

Quincy thought for a moment of what he should say versus what his heart knew to be true. When he figured Josie belonged to another man, he had kept a polite distance. The night they shared didn't matter. She'd been a lady before, and she was a lady afterward. The Morgan farm loomed up ahead, their big red barn standing bright from between the trees surrounding the homestead. If he didn't tell her his feelings now, he might never have the guts or the chance again. "Yes, even if you would go home with another man immediately after. I didn't care how, but I needed either to say goodbye one last time and make sure you would be safe tonight."

"I like how you care so much for me."

"It's impossible not to adore you." He waited, hoping she'd add to the conversation, say something about how she had growing feelings for him. She remained quiet and seemed more interested in the landscape than in him. Unwilling to go any longer in silence, compelling her to refuse or dismiss his affections, he pointed and redirected their conversation to safer ground. "See? Another half mile, and we'll be there. In fact, I'll be surprised if they don't already know we're here."

"Did they know you'd visit today?"

"Yes, I'd wanted to make sure everyone was happy with the arrangement." Each roll of the wheels, every hoof step, took them closer to the family. The motions also brought him closer to realizing she couldn't hold the same affection for him.

Josie looked all around them as they rode closer to the main house. "The place seems rather quiet. I expected the boys to be running out to us by now." As he pulled the buggy to a halt in front of the Morgan home, she asked, "Do you suppose they forgot the day?"

"I hope not." He hopped down from the buggy and reached out to help her. "I was very clear about leaving for Chicago tomorrow morning." She stumbled a bit, pressing her hand against his chest to steady herself. He sucked in a breath at the touch. Warmth radiated from her palm throughout his body. "Josie—" he began.

"We need to find Jake, Mike, and the Morgans, remember?"

Despite their heated contact, her words were a cold bucket of ice dumped over his head. She may enjoy his company, but she didn't love him. He nodded, trying to give her a smile. "Of course. Let's see where they are."

Quincy fought the urge to let her hold his arm. As they approached the front porch, a warning went down his spine. The door was ajar. Not much, but enough to signal something was very wrong. "Stay here. If I yell, run back to the buggy and hurry back to town."

She followed close behind. A board squeaked under her weight. "But, I don't want to—"

He cut her off. "I don't care." She was too good of a person to just leave someone in trouble behind, so he appealed to her better nature so she'd go to safety. "You'll get help if I need it. Agreed?"

"All right."

Ignoring her surly tone, he entered the house. Quiet filled the area. He listened for noises for several seconds. Nothing. The only breathing he heard was his and Josie's. "Come on," he whispered. "I don't think anyone is in the house."

She closed the door behind them, the soft click loud in the silence. "What do we do now?" she said, barely audible. "What if they went into Sacramento to find you?"

"I'd be inclined to agree except the front door being open. Their being so negligent worries me." He stepped farther into the foyer, looking up the stairwell. "I'm going to holler for them," he said. "Hello? Chuck? Mrs. Morgan? Is anyone home?"

Neither moved as he waited for an answer. Josie tapped him on the arm. "Do they work in the fields, or are there servants to do that for them?"

"From what I gathered, they have employees of all kinds." Continuing through the house, he added, "Looks like Mrs. Morgan doesn't have servants or gave them the day free."

The back door was also slightly open, so Quincy

stepped through. Josie did as well, grabbing his arm. "Quince, hear that?" She stood frozen in her spot. "Listen."

He strained and caught the faint screams. Fear raced through his nerves like static in a thunderstorm. "Get inside and lock up," he ordered before running toward the cries.

Not until he'd passed a bunkhouse, corral, and several animal pens did he see the commotion. Quincy slumped against a tree in relief at seeing everyone safe. Instead of someone attacking the Morgan family, Mike merely splashed in a creek with Chuck while Nancy swung Jake to let his feet skim the water.

Chuck paused his water fight with Mike to wave at Quincy. "Hello there. We'd just about given up on you."

"I can see that." He nodded at Nancy. "Ma'am."

She laughed, swinging Jake to perch on one hip. "Sorry to be in such a state. I couldn't resist joining in."

He held out his hand to help her up the bank. "No need to apologize. I completely understand." He'd never played in a creek as a child. Jake and Mike, now on the shore with his new father, would have the loving family every orphan longed for.

Chuck clapped him on the back, holding Mike to keep the boy from hugging Quincy. "Let's get everyone presentable for you and continue this visit in dry clothes."

Nancy fell in step with Quincy behind her husband. "I can fix a quick lunch if you're hungry."

"Please?" Mike asked.

"Certainly," Nancy replied. "Let's let Chuck clean you up while I set the table."

Chuck looked back at him. "Mr. Easton, I see you brought a friend."

He saw Josie standing on the back porch, her hands on her hips and smiling. "I did." Sunlight gave her hair a golden shine. As they approached, her smile widened. She knelt, holding her arms out to the boys.

"Josie!" Mike yelled and ran to her before anyone could stop him. The boy clung to her, only letting go when the other adults approached.

Just as Quincy had feared, the boy had soaked Josie's dress. "Oh no," Nancy exclaimed next to him. "I'm so sorry."

She chuckled. "No need to be. I could use a good scrubbing."

"Nancy and Charles, this is Josie Simmons," Quincy began.

Mike took over the introductions, hopping up and down. "We met her on the way out here. She helped Mr. Easton take care of us."

Nancy's eyebrows rose. "Oh, did she?"

Quincy couldn't let them think poorly of her. "Miss Simmons was a mail-order bride, but her plans went awry. The boys had grown fond of her, so I invited her out to visit them before I went home." He gave her a slight smile, not wanting to tell the truth about Will's deception or his unreturned feelings for her. Yet he was unwilling to lie even to himself. He forced out the words, "She and I are mere acquaintances who'll go our separate ways when we leave here."

CHAPTER 12

Josie stared at Quincy. Had he just implied they were nothing more than friends even after their kiss this morning? Maybe he'd merely touched the back of her hand with his lips, but still. It was a kiss. She tried to smile, stammering, "Very true."

Mrs. Morgan stepped up, crooking her finger in a follow-me motion. "Chuck can assemble a lunch while I find you something dry to wear. I used to be your size." Josie trailed behind as Nancy led her out of the room and upstairs. "Anything I'll give you will be woefully out of fashion, but you can change back once your dress is dry."

"I do have something else to wear." She continued down the hallway with Nancy, getting a glimpse of the boys' bedroom. The fabrics were colorful, and toys were strewn all over. Happy to see the children so well provided for, she continued her protest. "It's no bother for me to retrieve and wear what I already own."

"It's also no bother for me to find a dress I can't fit into that compliments your coloring far better than gray does." She opened a trunk at the foot of her and her husband's bed. "Everything in here is too tight, yet I didn't have the heart to use them as rags." She pulled one dress after another out, laying them on the bed.

Josie marveled at the fabrics. Farming must provide a better living than she'd ever expected. "You can't let me have any of these. They're all too beautiful."

She held up one of the garments in front of Josie as if she were a paper doll. "Their loveliness is exactly why I need to give you at least one." Setting it aside, she did the same with a green dress with white lace. "This will be perfect, but there are a couple more I'd like to check."

"I don't know what to say about so much generosity."

Nancy laughed. "Thank you with a smile comes to mind." She gave Josie the white laced green dress to hold. "Here. Try this on and come get me while you're in it. I'll need to put the boys in fresh clothes and check on Chuck to make sure he's not destroying my kitchen."

Before she could agree, Nancy was gone. Her everyday dress wasn't soaked through. Not enough to justify taking another woman's cast-offs. Yet…she held the dress up to her. Nancy had a refined taste Aunt Erma had never allowed

Josie to have. Her bag held space for only one dress, not two or the five Nancy had laid out. Still, maybe one made of thin satin might fit? She began undressing. She let the green dress fall over her head and turned to look in the dresser mirror.

Taking a few steps closer, she gazed in wonder at how beautiful she was. Her thinking such a thing was the height of vanity for sure, yet, no other words described how her eyes, skin, and hair glowed. Even her Sunday best dress, though green too, didn't make her radiant like this shade did. She let down her tresses to arrange them better. What would Quincy's reaction be to her appearance? Would he agree on how Nancy was right? Josie lifted her chin and smiled. The color vastly improved her appearance.

She slipped on her shoes and went to the kitchen. Walking down the stairs in such a delicate dress left her feeling like a true lady of the manor. Voices from the kitchen stopped her. Quincy's voice vibrated through her like the perfectly tuned piano key. She took a few steps closer, ashamed of herself for falling in love with him so quickly. Trying to resist him today had failed miserably. Besides, hadn't she learned from her mistake with Will? Except, she'd met Quincy in person and not through a lot of letters and lies. The circumstances between the two men weren't even close to being the same.

Shaking off the doubt filling her head, Josie walked into

the kitchen. The room fell silent as everyone stared. Her cheeks burned as she said, "You were right, Nancy. This dress is perfect." She gave a shy glance at Quincy. When their eyes met, he closed his mouth as if caught agog. "It's far prettier than my usual work dresses."

In fresh clothes, Jake toddled over to her, wrapping his arms around her skirted legs. Mike did the same, and she laughed. "I'm glad you're both dry this time."

Nancy motioned toward an empty chair. "Sit down and eat, so later we can have you try on other dresses."

"I don't know. If I spill something on this..." Josie ventured. "It's almost too pretty to wear."

Mike held up a napkin. "You can do what I do and tuck this in your neck."

She glanced at Quincy first for clarification. He grinned, saying, "Like a makeshift bib."

Josie ruffled Mike's hair. "That's an excellent idea," she said as Quincy led him and the younger child to their seats. Canned fruits, biscuits, and sliced cheeses had been arranged on a platter in the center of the table. Two of the chairs didn't match the other four. She smiled, thinking of how the Morgans had planned for the boys before they'd arrived.

Chuck cleared his throat while his wife dished up the children's plates. "I was telling Mr. Easton how you caught us at a bad time earlier, Miss Simmons. Usually, we're working, but with the boys arriving yesterday, I gave my hired help the afternoon off."

Nancy chimed in. "I encouraged him to let us have time as a family because our boys need both of us."

"And we need them," Chuck added. "I wanted to leave the farm or at least what it's worth to my children. Years passed, and we were never blessed."

"I didn't want to wait anymore," his wife said. "After seeing news of all the children lacking a good home, we knew what we had to do."

Quincy wiped his mouth, his gaze never wavering from Josie's. "I don't blame you. Everyone hopes to leave a legacy to their family someday. I grew up without parents, without a family of my own, yet I want to give whatever legacy I build to my sons or daughters someday."

Chuck beamed at him. "I'm sure you will, son. You're a fine young man doing wonderful work for the orphanage."

"Thank you," Quincy said. "I enjoy my work and the lives I change for the better."

She swallowed the last bite of spiced peaches on her plate, her stomach full of butterflies. He wanted to keep doing his work, which was commendable, but how did he plan on starting a family while traveling so much with orphans? If she had a husband like Quincy, she'd want him home with her all the time.

Before she could further ponder Quincy's plans for his

future, he stood. "Chuck, Nancy, you have provided Michael and Jacob with a good home and family." Shaking Chuck's hand, he added, "It's been my pleasure to ensure the boys have you two for parents."

Nancy wiped tears from her eyes, and as Josie stood, she couldn't help but do the same with the bib Mike had provided her. Nancy said, "You're a gift, truly, and thank you for introducing Miss Easton—" She stopped, her face reddening. "Excuse me, I mean, Miss Simmons. It's been a pleasure playing dress-up with her."

"You're welcome. I'm lucky she'll go along with a mongrel like me," he quipped.

Josie couldn't let him get away with the self-deprecating comment. "Don't be silly. I know a cur when I meet him, and you're not one at all."

Mike yawned, and Chuck scooped him up in his arms. "I know a couple of boys who could use a nap."

Nancy nodded in agreement as she picked up Jake, too, and said to Josie, "Let's find you another dress, Miss Simmons, so you two can get back to town sooner rather than later."

She nodded as the older lady handed the boy to Quincy. "If you're sure. This and your other cast-offs are so pretty."

The older lady led the way back upstairs again. "I'm very sure. I'd prefer a lovely young woman should wear them again than they end up as moth food later." She knelt, digging in the trunk once more. "There's something I have in mind for you. It'll be light for the summer." Pulling out a dark cream dress, she stood. "And there it is. I wore this when I was your age for special events." She held the garment out to Josie, who took the dress from her. "I don't think you'll need to try it on for the fit, but I'd love to see how the color looks on you."

The satin slid across her fingertips. "Are you sure? This seems too special for me."

"I'm positive. We have boys, and I can't wear anything so small anymore. Farm life gives a woman curves she never expected." Nancy headed for the door. "I'll be waiting outside."

As soon as the latch clicked shut, Josie shed the beautiful green dress in favor of the lighter colored one. Even tugging the garment over her head seemed too harsh for such a delicate fabric. She stepped in front of the mirror. How Nancy knew what looked good on her amazed Josie. The woman must have been a dressmaker in a former life. She turned first one way and then another, enjoying how the pale yellow satin shimmered. The material could be folded small enough to fit in her carpetbag, and since Nancy insisted? She'd gladly take the dress home despite Aunt Erma's disapproval. "All right, I'm ready."

The door opened, and Quincy peeked in. "Are you

sure?" he asked first, then said, "Oh my," when he fully saw her. His mouth hung open for a second or two before he thought to close it.

"Where's Nancy?"

"Jake was fussy. I thought her attending to him would be better than my doing so." He walked in, still staring at Josie. "Let him attach to her instead of me." He circled her. "You were beautiful in your ordinary dress earlier today. Then, the other green at lunch complimented you more, which I didn't think was possible."

"And now?" She ran her hands over her hips, the fabric clinging to her curves. "You don't think this is too much for me?"

"No. It's perfect. I've never seen anything more beautiful in my life than you standing in front of me."

Her cheeks burned. "Pshaw, you probably have. Roses, sunsets, lots of things."

"Lovely, all of them, but not as perfect as you are." He leaned in, brushing her lips with his own. Without breaking their contact, he murmured, "I liked you the moment I saw you. I adored you the moment we first spoke. I loved you the moment you hugged Mike and Jake in their bunk." Deepening their kiss, he held her in his arms.

She closed her eyes, the sensation of being complete too much to bear. Putting her hands on Quincy's arms, his muscles under the cotton shirt seemed strong enough to hold her forever. He was a man who would keep her safe and cared about her happiness. Breaking away first, she smiled up into his slightly dazed expression. "All of a sudden, I'm glad I'm not married right now."

"Would you ever want to be someone's wife?"

"Just someone's?" she questioned and laughed. "No." Before his smile faded much more, she added, "No, I would only want to be your wife."

Relief relaxed his face. "Miss Simmons, are you proposing to me?"

Unable to help herself, she gave him a quick kiss, only stopping to say, "I do believe I am. Since my being proposed to didn't work out, I've decided to take charge. If you marry me, I'd love to be your wife."

He tilted his head, his eyes narrowing. "Would you mind traveling with me? Delivering children to good homes all over the country?"

"Yes, up to a point," she teased, trying to not giggle at the one reason why she'd balk over seeing the country with him.

He frowned. "Which is?"

"When I start having our babies, I'd like both of us to stay home more."

Quincy picked her up in a hug and swung her around with a whoop. "It's a deal, Miss Simmons. I'll marry you anytime you'd like."

"Should we tell the Morgans that I'll be wearing this as a wedding dress in the next couple of days?"

"Yes, after this." He lifted her chin a little, kissing both sides of her mouth before capturing his lips with hers. Josie felt the promise of his love deep in her bones and felt the same about him. Putting her arms around his muscular body, she held the love of her life intending to never let him go.

Thank you for reading Quincy and Josie's love story! If you enjoyed this book, please consider sharing the love and leave a review. Check out the About the Author section for more information on keeping in the loop on new books for you.

You *have* read Last Train Home, haven't you? Just in case you haven't, here's a little bit of Jack and Alice Dryden's romance and how they met.

LAST TRAIN HOME

THE AMERICAN WEST SERIES — BONUS MATERIAL

JACK DRYDEN STARED OUT THE DIRTY WINDOW, CHIN resting on his hands as if in prayer. He shivered. The midmorning sun barely affected the frost. Last night's fire in the woodstove remained cold and silent behind him. His wife, Ellie, had been gone three weeks, or was it four by now? His days blended into one blur since she'd left.

He did happen to remember the orphans arrived today. Sending a letter canceling the adoption hovered at the top of his chores. Yet Jack didn't have the heart to even write the message, never mind the ride to town and send it. "You picked a hell of a time to leave," he growled, as if she'd hear him while at home in Boston.

The papers lay on the table in front of him and reflected the morning light from the window. One's handwriting held the graceful curve of his runaway wife with a formal and final goodbye. The page covered a divorce decree for him to sign. His gut churned yet again. Wives didn't divorce their husbands. He'd meant it when vowing until death do them part, even if she hadn't.

Jack scratched the back of his neck. Their love might have faded to tissue-thin over the years, but he still respected his wife. He folded both papers, his signature blank, vacant and nagging at him. After a couple of seconds, he tucked in the envelope flap. Ellie had left because of him and not for anyone else. He reckoned neither one of them was in a hurry to make the document final.

The typewritten notice of the instant family he'd requested several months ago now sat on top. He sighed. No need to rush over to the courthouse after telling the orphans he'd not be able to adopt them after all. He had enough bad news to deliver already. Unable to leave it alone, Jack pulled the official letter from its envelope and stared at the enclosed photo.

The Children's Society had sent the information about the girl and twin boys soon after Ellie's departure. He narrowed his eyes. If she'd waited a couple of weeks to leave him, the orphans and his wife might have passed each other on the way to the children's new home. Jack wondered what Ellie might say if seeing them in a depot while they waited for the train to him. What could she say? "Sorry, but I'm not your mother or your father's wife after all"? Judging by her goodbye letter, Ellie wouldn't have the guts to say the words. He snorted. Maybe pin a note to their lapels, but that's all.

He looked over the photo, not bothering to reread the date written on the back. The sadness in the children's eyes told him everything. The girl stood behind the boys, a hand on each of the twins' shoulders. Jack couldn't help but smile, recognizing the protectiveness of an older sibling. In the image, the trio seemed well taken care of, and maybe they had been before their parents' deaths.

Jack slid the photo back into the envelope. A black and white image said nothing about hair or eye color. Still, the nuns had waxed poetic about the blonde hair and blue eyes of all three and how lucky he was to get such beautiful children to raise. He grunted and pushed aside both letters on the table. A person's looks didn't matter to him right now. Ellie proved to him that a pretty outside never meant a pretty inside.

He stood, the chair's legs scraping along the dusty wood floor. The place wasn't ready for more than the meager livestock he had, never mind new family members. Jack grabbed his coat and hat on his way to the door. He'd ride into town, tell the nuns he couldn't take the orphans after all, and be done with the matter. Maybe live another year out here and get the homestead ready to sell. No need to stay and build a family farm when Ellie had taken his heart back to Boston.

Once outside, a hard breeze cut through his coat. The early winter sky's pale blue matched the icy air. Jack hoped his horse, the one Ellie had left him, would move better in the cold than he did.

He walked up to Shep's stall in the barn and paused. The animal nickered, and Jack grinned. "Hey boy," he said, coming up to the animal and running a hand along his neck. "Feel like going into town?" As if answering him, the horse nudged his arm. Jack chuckled and said, "All right. Let's go." He led Shep out of the stall.

The buggy sat to one side of the wagon, and he paused. Riding would be faster, but he might need more than saddlebags after stopping by the dry goods store on his way home. "I suppose hitching the buggy wouldn't hurt," Jack muttered and reached for the bridle. "It'll keep me from visiting the saloon for some Christmas cheer, right, buddy?" The horse nickered when Jack gave him another scratch between the ears. Some men left their wagons tied to the post outside the saloon in any weather. He'd wanted to unhitch all the suffering animals and care for them like they deserved.

He soon had the horse fastened up and ready to go. Leading the animal past the house before getting onto the wagon reminded Jack he might need the orphanage's letter after all. "Give me a minute, boy," he muttered and hurried into the house to scoop up both letters. Ellie's goodbye would be proof to the caretaker that the children would be better off with anyone but him. He shoved the envelopes into a coat pocket.

His footsteps on the frozen blades of grass almost drowned out the papers' crinkling as Jack went to Shep. He double-checked the rigging and planned to reread Ellie's goodbye one more time before writing a final plea for her to return home to him. He paused for a moment before digging leather gloves out of his other coat pocket.

A contrary voice inside of him piped up about how she'd refuse him yet again. A smart man would have the papers signed and delivered by now. He shook his head, intent on dealing with the divorce later. Once on the buggy seat, he clicked to Shep. "C'mon, boy. Let's get this over with."

🚂

ALICE MCCARTHY SQUEEZED THE HANDBAG'S handles. Her first trip so far west to Liberty, Missouri, couldn't go awry now. She glanced at the eldest child, Charlotte, and smiled in reassurance while saying, "Mr. Dryden will be here soon. We're early, that's all." Worry faded from the girl's blue eyes, and her shoulders relaxed.

Charlotte shifted her belongings to the other hand and wrapped a blonde curl around her now freed finger. "I hope so. They do want us, don't they?"

"Of course, they do," Alice assured her. She kept a watch over the twins as they played tag around the railroad depot's rosebushes. Charlotte's twelve years to the boys' ten wasn't a huge age gap, and she smiled. Their difference in maturity meant the girl paced from nervous energy with her instead of dirtying her clothes while playing. Alice took a couple of steps toward the edge of the train station platform, and said, "Boys, be careful to stay neat. We want to impress Mr. and Mrs. Dryden, not scare them."

"Yes, Miss McCarthy," they chanted in unison. One of them wiped dirty hands on his pants, leaving limestone-white streaks on dark fabric.

"Oh, Conner." Alice sighed and reached for her handkerchief. "Come on over and let me clean you up. The Drydens should be here at any moment."

The boy did as she requested with Carter following him. Charlotte dropped her bag next to her brothers' and crossed her arms while tapping her foot. Alice hid a smile at how well the girl mimicked Sister Theresa's mannerisms. Good thing they weren't in the Children's Home at the moment, or the Sister might take it personally.

"There." Alice gave his trousers a final swipe of her

handkerchief. "All better." She straightened. "Be careful to not let the thorns snag on anything."

Neither boy replied but ran back to resume their game. She shivered and turned to the young girl. "Let's walk around again to keep warm."

Charlotte nodded, and both picked up the boys' carpetbags. The two stepped off the platform and into the winter sun's warmth. Alice checked the time on the depot's clock before they turned the corner. They'd been here two hours with no Drydens. People backed out of taking in children all the time. She'd have to contact the town's children placement board members at some point. Let them make suggestions on the best parents for the Hays children.

She chewed on a small chapped piece of her lower lip. Alice had reviewed the Drydens' application herself, along with acquiring Sister Theresa's final approval. So many people needed help on the farm, and the couple seemed like reliable, decent folks. Not the type to miss meeting new family members for the first time.

Neither woman hurried for the shady side of the station, nor did she and Charlotte talk. While the girl was naturally quiet, Alice wanted to stall chatting with her about putting the three of them up to the community at large. Give the prospective parents a little while longer, just in case.

"They're not coming for us, are they?"

She paused in mid-step at the girl giving voice to Alice's worries. "Oh, I wouldn't say that. They might be delayed for some reason. The farm is a half-day's ride, remember."

Charlotte nodded, and they continued walking to the far side of the depot and out of the warmth. "I'd like to believe that, but it's late afternoon."

"I know. Everything will be fine, I promise." She smiled, ignoring the guilt smothering her heart. Alice could guarantee nothing, really, except she wouldn't abandon this family. The sisters at the Home encouraged keeping siblings together, but sometimes separations couldn't be helped. She glanced at Charlotte. She had shifted to holding everything with one hand and toyed with her hair again. The girl had a curl wrapped around her index finger so tight, the skin was a reddish-purple. Alice shared her fear and placed a hand on her slight back. "Even if the Drydens have changed their minds, you're not to worry. I'm here to help you and the boys find a good home."

They turned the corner, and both halted when seeing the boys hugging a man as if they were never letting go. When he glanced up at the ladies, Alice's heart stopped as she stared into the greenest eyes she'd ever seen.

The mystery man had several days' beard as black as his midnight hair. A hat pressed low over his forehead gave him an intense appearance, even if the dark curls hinted at the more boyish aspect of him. His clothes looked a little too lived in, and she wondered what wife would let her husband go to town in a rumpled shirt and pants. His coat and boots had some wear as well.

Finished with her appraisal, she glanced up into his eyes again. His slight smile led her into giving him one of her own. He awkwardly patted each child on the back, his expression silently begging her for assistance. Alice swallowed and took a step forward. "Hello, it looks like you need some help."

The twins flanked him, holding on as if he were a tree during a hurricane. He gave her a slight grin. "I do, please," he responded while putting a hand on each boy's shoulder.

The man's deep and even voice did fluttery things to her heart, and her face filled with heat. She'd met so many men in the past year of helping children find homes. This one beat out anyone she'd ever met before, and Alice cleared her throat to collect herself. "This raucous behavior won't do, boys." What if the couple showed to take the children home and saw them clinging to strangers? "Come along. Let the gentleman go."

Before she could step up and pull the twins away, Charlotte squeaked out a sob. "Pa? Is that really you?"

Continue reading Last Train Home on Amazon

ABOUT THE AUTHOR

With an overactive imagination and a love for writing, I decided to type out my daydreams and what ifs. I currently live in Kansas City with my husband and a few cats. When not at the computer, I'm supposed to be in the park for a jog and not buying everything in the yarn store's clearance section.

Find me online at:
https://twitter.com/LauraLStapleton
https://www.facebook.com/LLStapleton
and at http://lauralstapleton.com.

Subscribe to my newsletter to keep up on the latest and join my Facebook group at Laura's Favorite Readers.

Printed in Great Britain
by Amazon